CUPID GOES TO GRETNA

CUPID GOES TO GRETNA

DEBORAH HALE

ISBN 978-1-989408-13-1

For my sister Cyndi Corscadden, whose charm
is matched only by her brains and beauty.

Chapter One

Bath, England 1815

"MR. ARMITAGE, WILL you please elope to Gretna with me?" Miss Ivy Greenwood asked in a breathless rush.

He must be dreaming. Surely he must be dreaming!

Oliver Armitage glanced up from his latest experiment and shook his head hard to dispel the vivid hallucination of the young lady standing in the open door of his study. This was what came of working thirty-six hours without a wink of sleep. Perhaps he should take better care of himself, as his aunt Felicity constantly urged.

This was not the first time Oliver had been vexed by dreams of beautiful, vivacious Ivy Greenwood. Nor was it the first time thoughts of her had interrupted his work. It was becoming a perfect nuisance!

"Oh please, Mr. Armitage, do not refuse until you have heard me out." Unaffected by the shaking of his head or the stinging slap Oliver delivered to his right cheek, the relentless mirage of Ivy Greenwood stepped into his study and closed the door behind her.

A fragrance wafted from her, sweetly at odds with the faint reek of chemicals in the room. Some floral distillation — *dianthus carophylius*, perhaps? Commonly known as clove-pink, the flower's oil was often used in compounding soaps.

Oliver had heard of overtired minds imagining sights and sounds, but never smells. She must be *real*!

"Miss Greenwood, what are you doing here?" He leaped

from his desk chair, trying to adjust his spectacles with one hand, while raking the other through his disheveled hair in a vain attempt to make himself presentable.

It did not work, or so Oliver judged by the look of pitied exasperation in Ivy Greenwood's eyes. Remarkable eyes they were, too, the precise melding of blue and green produced by the combustion of copper. Looking into them produced a curiously combustible sensation in Oliver Armitage.

"What am I doing here?" The lady echoed his question. "I told you straight away, or did you not hear me? I need you to elope with me to Gretna Green. The happiness of your aunt and my dear brother depend upon it. Please, will you help me?"

Oliver's fatigue-addled mind struggled to fathom what she was talking about. At the same time a number of alarming sensations diffused through his chest, provoked by the notion of wedding this baffling, bewitching creature.

"I must confess myself at a loss, Miss Greenwood." Intellect being his sole source of pride, Oliver shrank from admitting his confusion. From the moment he'd met her, the young lady had confused him on far too many levels for his liking. "While I would like to oblige you, I have no intention of marrying you or anyone else, no matter how greatly Aunt Felicity may desire it."

"But she does *not* desire it — that's the whole point." Ivy Greenwood swept a glance around the makeshift laboratory Oliver had set up in the guest room of his Aunt's townhouse. Perhaps she thought he could use a wife to impose a little order on the scientific clutter. "I assure you, I have no intention of compromising your bachelor state, sir. Let me explain myself better. My brother and sister understand me so well that I fear I have fallen into the lamentable habit of jumping into the middle of a discussion and expecting other people to follow me."

A trill of laughter at her own expense shook Miss Greenwood, making the lustrous curls that peeped out from under her bonnet dance. Their hue put Oliver in mind of a freshly burnished copper-gold alloy.

"Pray have a seat while you explain." As he scooped a pile of books and papers off the nearest armchair, Oliver wondered why the news that Ivy Greenwood had no designs on his bachelorhood did not prompt the anticipated surge of relief.

"Thank you, Mr. Armitage." She gave the embroidered chair seat a rather doubtful look before perching on the edge of it. "Now, let's see ... begin at the beginning. I don't want to go too far back, or it will take me ages to tell, and we haven't much time."

"Perhaps if you would clarify the points on which I am confused." Oliver lowered himself back onto his desk chair, belatedly wondering if his cravat might be hopelessly stained with the residue of mineral salts. "You wish us to elope, but not get married. That is a contradiction, you must admit. And what do Aunt Felicity and your brother have to do with this eloping business?"

"That's it!" A smile of blinding intensity lit Ivy Greenwood's delicate features. For an intoxicating instant she regarded him with a look of dazzling admiration, as though he had just unlocked the secrets of the universe for her. "I expect you know that your aunt has been my brother's mistress for the past two months."

The shock of hearing her speak so casually of such scandalous matters made Oliver's lips open and shut rapidly, without engaging his other vocal organs.

Ivy Greenwood ignored his mimicry of a beached fish. "I have never seen my brother happier than he has been lately. Watching them together, I am convinced your aunt was quite as smitten with Thorn as he was with her."

Oliver managed a nod. Though not as perceptive of human emotions as Miss Greenwood appeared to be, he had sensed a change in his Aunt Felicity. It had seemed to him as if the twelve-year difference in their ages had narrowed further still, making him the senior of the two. For that reason, Oliver had warmed to Hawthorn Greenwood as he had to few other men — including his Uncle Percy, Lady Lyte's first husband.

"If you and I can see how well suited they are, how can Thorn and your aunt be so blind to it?" Ivy Greenwood demanded.

"You are losing me again." Oliver strove to concentrate his weary wits on what the lady was saying, instead of how her eyes sparkled or the way she cocked her head to one side when she spoke, like a winsome little bird. "How can you be certain they *are* blind to it?"

"Be-cause," she explained with the exaggerated patience of a school mistress tutoring a particularly backward scholar, "she gave poor Thorn his marching orders yesterday."

"Oh dear."

"Oh dear, indeed." Ivy Greenwood's voice sharpened. "Without a word of warning or explanation that I could tell. Thorn is wandering around in shock, as though he'd been hit by a runaway mail coach. If I did not like your aunt so well, I would be furious with her for treating him so badly."

As he tried to digest this information, Oliver found himself wishing someone cared enough to be as indignant on his behalf as Miss Greenwood was for her brother. "Now would you kindly explain how Gretna Green figures into all this?"

Since the introduction of Lord Hardwick's *Marriage Act*, some sixty years before, couples desiring to wed against their families' wishes often fled to Scotland, where matrimonial law was scandalously lax.

"It is quite simple, really." Miss Greenwood treated Oliver to a most disarming smile. "I am certain that all Thorn and your aunt need is a little time and privacy to sort out whatever has gone wrong between them. But I know my brother. If he thinks Lady Lyte wants nothing more to do with him, he would never impose upon her, which may be exactly what she wishes he *would* do."

Oliver rubbed his brow, behind which he could feel a vicious headache brewing. He doubted whatever else Ivy Greenwood had to say would prove soothing.

As she watched the young scientist massage his forehead, a mystifying urge overtook Ivy. Never one to resist an impulse, she sprang from her chair and knelt beside his. Reaching up, she pushed an unruly lock of chestnut hair from his brow. "Are you ill, Mr. Armitage?"

The hazel gaze he turned upon Ivy unsettled her. It was plain to see the man did not take proper care of himself. For the first time in her life, she yearned to look after someone.

Her precipitous arrival and non-stop chatter could not have done the poor fellow any good. "I probably oughtn't to have barged in on you like this. But when the idea came to me, I *knew* it might be the only chance for Thorn and I had to act upon it without delay. I suppose that sounds quite ridiculous to you."

"O-on the contrary, Miss Greenwood." Though he appeared alarmed by her nearness, Oliver Armitage did not move away. "It is the first thing you've said that I understand completely. Sometimes when I have been brooding over a particular experiment, I will get a sudden flash of insight into what is happening or how I could do it differently. Then I cannot rest or sleep or eat until I have tested my theory."

An eager smile seemed to take his angular features as much by surprise as it took Ivy. If he spruced himself up and made an effort to look less sober and serious all the time, Oliver Armitage might have a bevy of young ladies pursuing him for more than his fortune.

His voice softened and for a dizzying instant his gaze played over her face like a caress. "What flash of inspiration has brought you to me, Miss Greenwood?"

For perhaps the first time in her life, Ivy found herself at a loss for words. All at once the notion of running off to Gretna Green with Oliver Armitage did not seem quite so comical. True, he mightn't be the kind of dashing rake she fancied, but there was something curiously compelling about him that she'd never appreciated until this very moment.

"When you first came in, you asked if I would elope with

you," he prompted her. "I still fail to see what that has to do with your brother and my aunt."

His admission freed Ivy's tongue from its unaccountable paralysis. "For a man who's supposed to be so clever, you don't understand very much about people, do you?"

His smile faded and a shadow darkened his eyes. "I fear you are correct. The human heart is one conundrum beyond my ability to fathom. Perhaps from so little practice."

For no reason that she could work out, Ivy suddenly felt ashamed. She almost blurted an apology for disturbing him and fled Lady Lyte's townhouse then and there. But she recalled the stricken look on Thorn's face when he had finished reading the letter from Oliver's aunt.

Dear Thorn had been mother and father to her since long before their father had died. Ivy would do anything to see him as happy again as he'd been during the last two months.

"What do you suppose your aunt would do if she discovered you'd set off for Scotland to marry some unsuitable young woman?" she asked Oliver Armitage.

He shrugged. "Try to stop me, I hope."

"Exactly!" Perhaps her plan had a chance of succeeding after all. If only she could win his cooperation. "Thorn would do the same if I eloped. I know he would. And what better opportunity for the pair of them to talk out their problems than on the long carriage ride to Scotland?"

Understanding flickered deep in his eyes and one corner of his wide mouth inched upward again. "You are proposing we stage a sham elopement in order to make your brother and Aunt Felicity follow us to Gretna?"

Ivy gave a vigorous nod. "Isn't it a stroke of genius? By the time they arrive, I expect they will be ready to step in front of a parson and take their own vows!"

Her enthusiasm for the whole project rekindled. "I have a natural talent for matchmaking, if I do say so. I managed to bring my sister Rosemary together with her destined husband. It was no easy task, either, what with her foolish pride and his unaccountable modesty. They are blissfully happy now, thanks to me, and I will not rest until I've done the same service for Thorn and your aunt."

"I approve of your goal, Miss Greenwood, but —"

"Do call me, Ivy, or Miss Ivy, if you must. Back in Lathbury, Rosemary was *Miss Greenwood* to everyone. Whenever I hear that name I want to check if my sister is standing behind me."

"Very well, Miss Ivy. About this scheme of yours —"

"Brilliant, isn't it?" Ivy almost hugged herself.

Another agreeable consequence of making this match between Thorn and Lady Lyte would be to bring Oliver Armitage into the Greenwood family. Once she got to know him better on this little jaunt to Gretna, she'd have an idea what sort of wife he needed. He struck her as just the sort of unassuming fellow who could use the help of an astute matchmaker like her.

For some reason, the notion of finding Mr. Armitage a wife did not elate her as she'd expected.

Ivy had no time to consider why that might be. "If we are to succeed we must act quickly, before Thorn and Lady Lyte have gotten used to being apart. Can you jot a note to your aunt and pack a portmanteau straight away?"

"Surely you must be —"

Another thought occurred to her. "Do you have a carriage of your own, or shall we need to hire a coach?"

"I have never felt the need of my own vehicle since Aunt Felicity has always lent me the use of hers."

"A rented coach it is, then. Thorn had to let all of ours go. They are such an expense to maintain." Ivy stifled a pang of regret. One could never count on hired transport to be as comfortable or reliable as a family's private equipage. Still, it was a small sacrifice to make for the sake of her brother's future happiness. "We must leave Thorn and your aunt the means to give chase as soon as they discover we've gone. We shall need money, too, I suppose, for coaches and inns and such. Do you have any? My dear brother-in-law gave me twenty whole pounds to kit myself out for the Season. I hardly spent any of it and this is a much more worthwhile enterprise, don't you think?"

Before she could say anything more, Oliver Armitage raised his hand and pressed his fingers over her lips with firm but gentle pressure. "Miss Greenwood ... Miss Ivy, please hear me out. Your goal is a laudable one, but you cannot be serious about this preposterous scheme. Your brother and my aunt are both past thirty — old enough to know their own minds, surely. We would do better not to meddle in a situation we may not fully understand. If either of them seeks our counsel, then we can offer our advice."

How dare he patronize her as if she was a silly child who could not comprehend the consequences of her actions? Ivy struggled to maintain her indignation while some foolish part of her enjoyed the sensation of his hand on her lips.

Just because Oliver Armitage had read all the thick, dusty tomes piled around the room, did not mean he knew *everything*. He'd confessed himself mystified by the workings of the human heart and on that account she felt sorry for him. She would rather understand about important things like love than have all the book learning in the world.

If Mr. Armitage believed he'd had the final say in all this, then the young scientist had made a grave miscalculation.

Chapter Two

OLIVER WOKE WITH a start, praying he would find himself
in his own bed or fallen asleep hunched over his desk.

Instead he discovered himself slumped on a hard seat
upholstered with dry, cracking leather, inside a bouncing,
swaying, rattling coach. A coach he vaguely recalled hiring
in Bath during what he'd hoped was a nightmare. How had
he let Ivy Greenwood talk him into such rash folly?

Almost against his will, Oliver's gaze strayed to the oppo-
site seat. The moment his eyes encountered the slumbering
form of Miss Greenwood, he found his answer in her beauty.

It was not an answer to his liking.

He prided himself on being a man of science, didn't he? A
man of science should collect facts and weigh them, then make
a rational decision based upon solid information. Dimples,
red-gold ringlets and eyes like shimmering aquamarines had
no place in such deliberations. Neither did that immeasurable,
intangible, thoroughly suspect quality known as *charm*.

Ivy Greenwood had *not* charmed him! Oliver's intellect
protested. She'd merely taken advantage of his exhausted
state, nattering on about love and happiness and family obli-
gations until he would have promised her anything to secure
a moment's peace. Now that he'd got a few hours' sleep to
shore up his will power, he would order this blasted vehicle
turned around and driven straight back to Bath before anyone
missed them, wouldn't he?

As he let his gaze linger over Miss Ivy, Oliver was not so
certain. In sleep her features had taken on a soft, ingenuous

caste that matched her temperament. Like a child, she was full to the brim with high spirits and sunny optimism, without a thought to spare for the harsh practicalities of life or the troublesome consequences of her impulsive actions.

Oliver could not help comparing her to the other young ladies he'd met in Bath — comely and controlled with a glitter of avarice in their eyes that no amount of fan fluttering could conceal. After their suffocating attentions, Ivy Greenwood had breezed into his life like a zephyr of clover-scented country air. No wonder such a singular creature had captured his interest.

Captured and held it hostage. That would never do, because Miss Greenwood was most definitely *not* a child. The bewitching curves beneath her light muslin gown were those of a woman, as were her ripe, inviting lips.

Oliver Armitage needed to concentrate all his mental powers upon his research, without feminine distractions. In short, he needed to purge Ivy Greenwood from his system. If there was an enterprise calculated to make him heartily sick of her, Oliver could think of none better than a tedious carriage ride of over three hundred miles.

Having satisfied himself with a sound, logical reason for continuing their journey, he settled back in his seat with a contented sigh and studied Ivy Greenwood as though she were some exotic botanical specimen. When a pedantic little voice in the back of his mind carped at his pathetic excuse for lingering in her company, Oliver told it to keep its opinions to itself.

<hr />

"Miss Ivy, wake up, will you?"

Ivy's fuzzy, half-asleep mind sensed she had been ignoring similar appeals for some time. This one sounded more insistent and more vexed than the ones before.

She gave a wide yawn and coaxed her eyes half open.

"I hope your bed curtains never catch fire while you're

asleep." A pleasant masculine voice betrayed just a hint of asperity. "You sleep as soundly as any hibernating animal."

"I'm sorry, Thorn." Ivy stretched then rubbed her eyes. "What time is it?"

"It is nearly sunset," replied the gentleman. "And I am not your brother. Luckily for you, he hasn't caught up with us ... yet."

Her eyes flew open. "Mr. Armitage!"

She glanced around the dim interior of the coach. "What ...? How ...?"

Her heart galloped faster than the faint beat of horses' hooves upon the highway as she struggled to marshal her wits. What *had* she done?

"We're in Gloucestershire." Oliver Armitage spoke in a calm, patient tone, though the crinkled line of his mouth suggested wry amusement at her expense. "Not far over the county line, but it is past time we put in somewhere to dine and sleep. Newport seems as good a place as any. Since it is on the provincial coach route north, we should have no trouble hiring fresh transport in the morning."

Dine? Sleep! The recollection of what she'd done slapped Ivy wide awake. The consequences of her folly threatened to overwhelm her.

"I know a good inn where we can take supper." Mr. Armitage sounded far more enthusiastic about the whole venture than when she'd first approached him. "We'd probably better not spend the night there, though."

Sleep with *him*? No wonder he looked so gratified all of a sudden. When she'd first hit on this plan, Oliver Armitage had seemed the perfect accomplice. Quiet, steady, bookish — just the sort of fellow with whom her virtue would be safe. Not a dashing young rogue who would tempt her and be tempted in turn.

Perhaps all men were rogues at heart. That enormous miscalculation dropped onto an already teetering pile which threatened to fall on Ivy and bury her.

"How could you let me go through with this?" she wailed. "Did you never stop to think what will happen if Thorn and your aunt *don't* come after us? This will all be for nothing. And my brother will probably call you out, or worse, insist that you marry me to salvage my reputation."

The notion of being tied for the rest of her life to an unromantic intellectual filled Ivy with dismay. "Why didn't you talk some sense into me? I have always been prone to speak and act before I think. But you are a man of science — you ought to have known better!"

"I did my damnedest to dissuade you, silly child!" In the gathering darkness, emerald lightning seemed to flash in Mr. Armitage's hazel eyes. His features took on a razor-sharp definition that was both frightening and stimulating to behold.

His voice echoed the raw crack of the coachman's whip. "I might just as soon have tried to talk a river out of flooding its banks, or warn a hurricane that it could unleash destruction. Did it ever occur to you that you should have staged this mock elopement with a man you *would* be willing to wed if worse came to worst?"

His outburst rocked Ivy back in her seat, speechless and strangely roused.

In the astonished silence that followed, she heard him mutter some words that he might not have meant to speak. "I know I am the last fellow in Bath a vivacious beauty would want for a husband. You needn't rub it in."

A nettle-sharp blush stung in Ivy's cheeks. Vivacious beauty — was that how he thought of her? Silly child had been nearer the mark. What a perfect little wretch she'd been! "Nonsense. I'm not half good enough for you."

Oliver Armitage had far more to lose in all this than she had. What if Lady Lyte did not make up her quarrel with Thorn? What if Oliver's aunt cut off his inheritance as punishment for taking part in this ridiculous escapade? Ivy knew she would never forgive herself.

Leaning forward, she reached across the narrow space

between their seats and grasped Oliver's hand. "I'm most awfully sorry for dragging you into this. And sorrier still for expecting you to talk sense into me when I should be taking responsibility for my own actions. How can I ever make it up to you?"

———⋙◆⋘———

Oliver stifled a grin. He didn't dare tell Ivy Greenwood what manner of compensation he found himself wanting from her.

Charm might be immeasurable and intangible, but he could not deny its existence. Nor the fact that Ivy possessed this mysterious power in ample quantity. How else could she have tempered his fury into indulgent amusement with a few disarming words of remorse and an impulsive squeeze of his hand?

One day science might unravel the riddle and translate it into a dry equation that made perfect sense, but Oliver hoped such a desecration would never come to pass in his lifetime.

At least Ivy Greenwood was forthright about not wanting any lasting attachment with him. Better that than playing the coquette and mouthing sentimental nonsense, all the while keeping a calculating eye trained on his bank balance.

"There, there." He patted her hand and released it … while he still could. "The situation is not as dire as all that. And you did not hold a cocked pistol to my head, forcing me to come with you. However ill-considered on both our parts, we are in this up to our necks now. If we mean to salvage anything worthwhile, we shall have to work together. Agreed?"

"Agreed." She heaved a sigh of relief. "You sound as though you have some plan of action in mind."

Off to the west, across the Severn and behind the Welsh hills, the May sun had set at last. Even though he could not make out Ivy's expression, Oliver sensed her interest focused upon him. Was there some force of personality akin to magnetism? he wondered.

"I propose we stop at the King's Arms in Newport and dine there. If my aunt does follow us, that is the first place where she is likely to stop and inquire. We often break our journey there when we travel between Bath and her house in the country."

Ivy clapped her hands. "You want to lay a clear trail for them to follow. How clever!"

The sincere ring of admiration in her voice went straight to Oliver's head, like a bolt of brandy on an empty stomach. He hadn't realized how intoxicating it might feel to be valued for himself rather than on account of the fortune he stood to inherit.

"That's not all." He resisted the urge to preen for her, but failed miserably. "While we dine, we must talk as if we plan to press on for Gloucester tonight. Perhaps make a point of asking the innkeeper where we can get fresh horses to continue our journey."

"But … we … won't?"

Oliver shook his head. "We need to be certain Aunt Felicity and your brother are following us. Otherwise, we might as well pack it in, head back to Bath and hope we can concoct a plausible story to avert a scandal."

Why didn't the prospect of extricating himself from this whole mess hold more appeal for him?

"I believe I see what you mean." Ivy's rising inflection told Oliver that she still did not follow him completely.

"We will spend the night across the way at the Green Dragon and keep watch," he explained. "Depending on whether your brother and Aunt Felicity turn up looking for us, we can decide how to proceed from there."

"A sound course, indeed." Her endorsement took on a somewhat doubtful tone. "When you say *spend the night*, what manner of sleeping arrangements did you have in mind?"

Thank heaven she hadn't waited to pose that question over supper. If he'd been partaking of beer or wine, Oliver feared he might have choked or expelled the libation out his nostrils!

As it was, he could blush and sputter under the benevolent cover of darkness.

"For a number of reasons, I think it best we share a room. If I can secure one with a window overlooking the street, that is. I doubt either of us will be much inclined to sleep after dozing in this coach all afternoon. Would you be agreeable to taking turns at watch? Say three hours at a spell. The one off watch may make use of the bed."

Ivy chuckled. "Is that what people mean when they say a lady and gentleman have *shared a bed*?"

"Miss Greenwood!" Oliver managed to squeak before his neck linen almost strangled him. He was already plagued by too many such thoughts without her taking pains to torment him.

"Oh, please don't let's be formal," she cajoled him. Despite his best effort to resist, Oliver could feel it working. "We are running away to Gretna, remember? And if our brilliant plan works as I'm certain it will, we'll soon be some sort of relations by marriage and then ..."

"Then?" He wasn't sure he liked the sound of that.

A flickering glow from the lighted windows of shops and houses told Oliver they must be driving into Newport. After conversing in darkness for some time, he could see Ivy's face clearly again. The sudden vision made him catch his breath.

How many young bucks in Bath would give up a year's allowance to trade places with him? None of them would be fool enough to take turns sharing a bed with such a winsome beauty.

A qualm of doubt wriggled deep in the pit of Oliver's belly. Would a close-quarter journey to the ends of the earth be sufficient to sicken him of Ivy Greenwood's sparkling company?

"Then?" He managed to ask again from a mouth gone dry.

Her eyes twinkled brighter than the evening stars. "Then I have brilliant plans for *you*, my dear Mr. Armitage."

Chapter Three

"My dear Mr. Armitage, that was as brilliant a performance as I've ever seen on the stage!" Two hours after their coach had rattled into Newport, Ivy concentrated to keep her words from sloshing around like wine in the bottom of a cup. "Every soul at the Kings' Arms from the hostlers to the waiter will be tripping over themselves to assure Thorn and Felicity that we drove off to Gloucester, tonight."

Her feet seemed much farther away than usual. It put Ivy in mind of her childhood back at Barnhill, staggering around the courtyard on a pair of stilts Thorn had built for her. Had she drunk too much, perhaps? The notion made Ivy chuckle to herself.

Unfortunately, she did not seem capable of laughing and walking at the same time. At least not with any amount of grace.

"Steady on, old girl." Oliver took her arm when she stumbled. "Perhaps I should take the first watch, so you can sleep this off."

She sagged against him with a grateful sigh. For such a clever boots, he really wasn't a bad old stick, particularly once he got outside a glass of wine and started to talk about his research. Much of it Ivy hadn't understood, but that only piqued her curiosity to find out more. As she primed him with question after question, Oliver Armitage fairly radiated his passion for discovery.

Animated and aglow, his features took on an appealing cast that caught Ivy by surprise. He would never be handsome in the manner that had previously caught her fancy — dark, devilish and dangerous. But there was a certain distinction about his well-shaped, expressive features and his alert, penetrating eyes that somehow dimmed the luster of those swarthy rakehells.

"The first watch?" It took her a moment of concentrated thinking to figure out what he meant. "Oh, *that* first watch. Of course. I shall have the bed well warmed for you when it comes your turn to sleep. You know, Oliver, you would be my perfect accomplice in all this, even if you weren't Lady Lyte's nephew."

They entered the Green Dragon Inn, where Oliver had secured them lodgings before taking her to dinner across the way. When he'd told the innkeeper they were newlyweds on their honeymoon tour, she had almost burst out laughing. Now the notion did not seem quite so comical.

"Perfect in what sense?" murmured Oliver, steering her up the narrow twisting stairs.

Ivy was grateful for his warmth, strength and steadiness.

"Perfect in playing the tactician to my strategist." She lolled against the wall as he opened the door to their room. "I dreamt up this lofty plan, as full of holes as a ruddy sieve. Then you wove in all the practical details to make it hold water."

"We do make rather a good team, don't we? I haven't the imagination to conceive of such an idea in the first place."

Oliver lit a candle that cast dancing shadows around the room. The chamber was so tiny it could barely hold the modest furnishings of a narrow bed, a washstand and a single chair.

Throwing off her bonnet and light shawl, Ivy reeled the few steps it took to carry her from the threshold to the bed then collapsed onto it.

"You don't have much of a head for drink, do you." Oliver pulled off her slippers and covered her with an extra blanket that lay folded at the foot of the bed.

As he drew it up over her shoulders, his hands lingered there for an extra second in something like a caress. Ivy wondered if he might press his lips to her brow in a goodnight kiss. When he pulled back at the last moment, then dragged the chair to the window and extinguished the candle, Ivy could not decide whether she felt relieved … or sorry.

⬛◆⬛

"Thorn used to tuck me in at night when I was a little girl." Ivy's drowsy murmur drifted out of the darkness behind Oliver.

He wished she would go to sleep. Then perhaps he could focus his thoughts on some scientific enigma, like the relationship between electricity and magnetism, and forget she was there.

He'd felt something rather like static electricity crackle between them this evening while they'd dined at the King's Arms. Her eager curiosity about his research had ignited a positive charge in their conversation that energized him. Now the knowledge that she lay so close by, soft, warm and languid, tugged on him with a force as powerful as ever a magnet had exerted on an iron nail.

"A strange duty for a brother," he mused, not certain if she was still awake to hear him. "Why would Thorn tuck you into bed rather than your mother or father?"

"I don't remember my mother." Did Ivy's sleepy words sound wistful, or was he reading his own feelings into them? "I'd barely been weaned when she died. Father always seemed to be off in London on some matter of business. We had servants, of course, but Thorn and Rosemary pretty much took charge of me. I sometimes think they gave up any kind of proper childhood for themselves to allow me one. That's why I do so want to help Thorn now, if I can.

"Such good times we had." In a soft, dreamy voice, Ivy wove a bright tapestry of words and wrapped it around Oliver, until he felt almost as if he'd taken part in her golden, carefree summers at Barnhill. Even the name of the Greenwood's estate in Buckinghamshire conjured up the scent of new mown hay and the distant lowing of cattle on a sun-drenched afternoon.

"What about you, Oliver?" she asked, at last. "Where is your home? What family do you have apart from your aunt?"

"None."

That sounded too bleak, too heavily weighted with self-pity, which was foolish since he never let himself dwell on it. "My father was an army officer in India. That's where I was born. I can still speak the odd word of Hindi I learned from my amah. My parents sent me to school in England as soon as I was old enough to make the journey. That climate is hard on English children."

In the shadow-wrapped street below, Oliver could picture his younger self howling and thrashing as strangers manhandled him aboard that ship bound for an impossibly distant land. His amah had knelt keening on the quay while his mother waved a handkerchief, her face almost as pale as that square of bleached cotton.

"Your parents aren't still in India, are they?" asked Ivy.

Oliver shook his head. "My father was killed in the Third Mysore War."

"I'm sorry."

"I wasn't. I scarcely remembered him. I was happy, because it meant my mother would come back to England."

After so long a pause he thought she must surely have fallen asleep, Ivy asked, "Did she?"

For the first time in almost twenty years he made himself say the words. "She drowned in a shipwreck on the voyage home."

Silently he begged Ivy not to offer sympathy. With the wine in his belly and his emotions stirred to a pitch he ordinarily took care to avoid, he might just break down and blubber a school boy's tears. The kind he used to hoard and only release a miserly few at a time, very late at night, like this. In dark, cramped, malodorous little rooms like this one.

He'd been a fool to let Ivy Greenwood beguile him into this madcap escapade! If only her brother and his aunt would stay put in Bath like sensible folk, he could trot her back there tomorrow and wash his hands of the whole enterprise.

Almost as if she could sense his thoughts, Ivy spoke. "Did you go to live with your aunt then?"

"Heavens, no!" Oliver pulled off his spectacles and dashed the back of his hand across his eyes. It came away only a little damp. "Felicity wasn't even my aunt, then. Now and again Uncle Percy would spare a thought for me — he was my mother's younger brother. Sometimes he would fetch me up to his house in Staffordshire for a bit of a holiday. I never could count on his remembering or scraping together the cash to finance it. Once he married Felicity he had plenty of money from her fortune. She was the one who arranged for me to come and stay with them at Christmas and every summer."

By then all the unshed tears had settled in his heart and frozen and he'd become a junior version of the man he was now — polite but insular, his nose buried in a book most of the time. With less than a dozen years' difference in their ages, Felicity had never tried to molly-coddle him. She had given him the first taste of real family life he'd ever known, though. He had developed a closer bond with her than with anyone else in England. It had grieved Oliver, in an abstract fashion, to watch her marriage sour when she could not provide his uncle with an heir.

More to herself than to him, he heard Ivy whisper, "I know my brother could make her happy, if only she would let him."

A mordant, mocking chuckle burst out of Oliver as he rose from his chair and stretched. "If only it were that simple."

Was he talking about Thorn and Felicity or about himself? Oliver wondered as he settled his spectacles back on his nose and scanned the deserted street once again. Surely it could not be as simple as letting a woman make him happy.

He could only imagine one who might be equal to the task. And he doubted she would be inclined to undertake it.

He snored! As the first feeble light of dawn stole through the inn's mullioned window, Ivy clapped a hand over her mouth to stifle a giggle. It seemed impossible that a paragon of intellect and decorum like Oliver Armitage should do something as *human* as belch or break wind ... or snore.

She rather liked the sound of it, though — a hushed, husky buzz that assured her he was sleeping peacefully. The poor fellow deserved a little peace after the upheaval she'd inflicted upon his tranquil life in the last eighteen hours. With one or two forgivable lapses, he'd been a jolly good sport about the whole madcap enterprise.

For a moment she turned her attention from the deserted street below to watch her travelling companion as he slept. Oliver rested on his side, his face turned toward her.

With his spectacles off and his features relaxed in sleep, Oliver Armitage looked years younger than his early twenties. Ivy could picture him in a schoolboy's high starched collar, his nose pressed against a frosty window, watching for a carriage that might fetch him away for the holidays. And when it failed to appear, hiding his face behind a book so no one might see the disappointment and longing in his eyes.

The thought of it gave her heart a queer twinge. Battling the urge to throw her arms around him and offer comfort that would be at least a dozen years too late in coming, Ivy forced her gaze back out the window.

There was still no sign of activity at the King's Arms. Might all her matchmaking come to naught, except to land her and Oliver into a boiling cauldron of scandal broth?

Behind her, Oliver mumbled something in his sleep and rolled over. The sounds somehow lured her gaze toward him again. This time he lay under the blanket in a boneless sprawl, his arms thrown wide. He'd peeled off his neck linen sometime in the night and the top few buttons of his shirt had come undone. The rumpled garment gaped open to expose a wedge of surprisingly muscular chest, lightly matted with fine dark hair.

If her inspection of his face had made her see the affection-starved little boy behind his unsociable facade, this glimpse of his bare chest reminded Ivy in most forceful terms that Oliver Armitage was a man grown.

She swallowed a lump that suddenly materialized in her throat. Had the stuffy little room gotten warmer all of a sudden? Perhaps the innkeeper had lit a fire downstairs. The urge to pitch herself onto the bed with Oliver reared once more, stronger than ever.

"Don't be such a goose, Ivy," she whispered to herself. "When you set out to find him a proper wife, a girl anything like *you* would be the last one to make your list of prospects."

Though she seldom heeded the voice of reason, this time Ivy found she could not ignore it. Why would she want to? The past day's excitement must be making her fanciful.

Her attention was so focused upon Oliver that at first she paid no heed to the muted noises in the street below. When at last she spared a glance back out the window, a fine barouche sat parked in front of the King's Arms. Could it be . . . ?

Elation vaulted her out of her chair and across the tiny distance to the bed.

Forgetting all her sister's warnings about waking sleepers gently, she grasped Oliver by the shoulders and shook him. "Wake up! I think they're here. Come tell me if that is your aunt's carriage!"

"What . . . ? Who . . . ?" He sat bolt upright, almost knocking his forehead against hers.

"A carriage just pulled up across the street," Ivy clutched his arm and dragged him toward the window. "I cannot imagine why anyone else would be abroad at such an hour. Is it your aunt's?"

Oliver's hand flailed out toward the washstand, snatched his spectacles and fumbled them onto his nose. He and Ivy pressed close together so they could both see out the tiny window.

"I do believe . . ." began Oliver.

Before he could say more, the familiar figure of a tall man opened the door of the barouche box and offered his hand to a familiar lady who emerged from within.

"It *is* them!" Ivy squealed. "Together!"

Relief surged through her like a powerful Atlantic gale, sweeping everything before it — sense, propriety, caution. She threw her arms around Oliver's neck kissing him with a force that surprised even her.

Chapter Four

FOR THE FIRST time since he'd set foot on English soil, over fifteen years ago, Oliver Armitage heeded the dictates of his heart rather than those of his head. When Ivy Greenwood hurled herself at him, her whole slender body fairly vibrating with joy and excitement, he did not resist the kiss she lavished upon him.

The pressure of her soft, warm lips overwhelmed his senses with a force that elated and alarmed him in equal measure. Not quite equal, perhaps. Elation came on at a swifter velocity, propelling his arms to close around her, his mouth to respond in a manner he'd never learned, but which somehow felt *right*.

His head tilted a fraction, to engage her more deeply. His lips parted, enticing hers to do likewise. One hand plunged into the silky floss of her hair while the other held her fast around the waist.

With the speed and energy of a violent chemical reaction, desire swept through him. His pulse raced and his nostrils flared, as though driven to consume as much air as possible to stoke the blaze within him. His head spun with a delicious dizziness, perhaps because all the blood in his body had rushed straight to his loins.

"Forgive me, Oliver!" As abruptly as she had flung herself at him, Ivy pulled away. "I let my excitement get the better of me."

She was not alone.

Her words doused Oliver as thoroughly as a pitcher full

of ice water over the head, allowing his tardy caution to catch and overtake him. Any power capable of shattering the barrier of reserve he'd labored for years to erect around himself was far too dangerous to meddle with.

Wrenching his hands away from Ivy, he put as much distance between them as the room's cramped quarters permitted. "I apologize for responding as I did. I must have been half-asleep still and fancied myself in a dream."

A rosy blush blossomed on Ivy Greenwood's fair face, but an impish grin arched her lips upward at the corners, calling forth a pair of devastating dimples. "You must have very … stimulating dreams, Mr. Armitage. I suspect you may be a man of hidden depths."

How dare she provoke such a powerful current of sensation within him, then turn around and laugh at him for surrendering to it?

"You find me amusing, Miss Greenwood?" He plucked his discarded stock off the floor and twined it around his neck almost as tight as a tourniquet. Perhaps that would keep the blood up in his head, where it belonged.

"Of course I find you amusing, and lots of other nice things besides." Refusing to be cowed by his icy tone or his sullen glare, Ivy once again disarmed him with her candor as she hunted up her slippers, shawl and bonnet. "I could not abide a man who didn't amuse me sometimes."

How could he stay angry when she appeared to mean it as a sincere compliment? And what "other nice things" did she find him besides amusing? While logic insisted he did not and should not care, his foolish curiosity fired all the same.

Determined to resist, Oliver turned the conversation to the one subject certain to distract her. "I must admit your plan to reunite Aunt Felicity with your brother appears to be succeeding. Last night, I would have rated the probability of their showing up together as very slight."

She responded to his words with the kind of luminous smile most women reserved for compliments on their appearance. Although it was pointless to compare any other woman's smile with that of Ivy Greenwood for she eclipsed them all with ease.

"You may know all about probability and other such subjects." Her eyes sparkled with the most engaging mischief. "Perhaps now you will admit I have certain insights into the mystery of the heart."

"Granted." He wished he dared ask her to explain the baffling emotions that tugged him in several different directions at once. Given that she was the one who provoked those emotions, perhaps it would be wiser to avoid the subject.

"Well?" Ivy nodded toward the window. "You said we should decide how to proceed once we discovered if they were following us. They are hot on our trail — together. After yesterday, I expect you want to march me across the street to Thorn and be done with it."

Part of him did, without a doubt. The considered, rational side that had ruled his life for many years. Another part, almost foreign to his nature, resisted the idea of abandoning this imprudent adventure and of parting from Ivy Greenwood a moment sooner than events made necessary.

Besides, there was Aunt Felicity to consider. He wanted to see her happy and on some distant level he sensed that Thorn Greenwood might well be equal to the task. For all her kindness to him, Oliver knew she was a strong-minded woman, not apt to be persuaded by ordinary means.

Ivy pulled a rueful face. "I must admit I had not taken into account all the bother involved in a journey to Gretna. I don't mind it for myself, but you will find it both uncomfortable and tedious, I expect. It was good of you to come this far with me after my brutal arm-twisting. If we continue, I want it to be *your* choice."

Risking a look into her eyes, Oliver saw reflected back an image of himself that he scarcely recognized. Once again he felt the subtle undercurrent of electricity, and the magnetic pull between two polar opposites of emotion and intellect.

"I suppose we might as well be hung for a sheep as a lamb." Though he tossed the words off in a casual tone, Oliver knew what a serious step he'd just taken.

He had made a commitment to this mad venture. He had made a commitment to this woman who represented a puzzle as challenging as any avenue of scientific inquiry. It was high time he dispensed with the illusion that this trip to Scotland would purge Ivy Greenwood from his system.

Unless he was very careful, he suspected her constant company might prove dangerously addictive.

"Life is going to seem rather dull after our little adventure, don't you think?"

As a fresh coach whisked them north to Tewkesbury, Ivy rummaged in a hamper of food she'd hurriedly purchased from the shops in Gloucester. Lifting out a golden-brown game pie, she passed it to Oliver on a napkin.

"Perhaps *my* life will," he replied, giving the pie an appreciative sniff. "I expect you make the dullest day an adventure for yourself and everyone around you."

Another man might have delivered that pretty compliment with a verbal flourish, but Oliver spoke with an earnest, self-conscious air that went straight to Ivy's heart.

Her mouth crammed with ham sandwich, she could manage no better reply than a lop-sided, cheek-bulging grin. True, she did her best to brighten life for herself and those around her. Nothing in ages had provided her such stimulation to equal her journey with Oliver Armitage.

Surely it was the thrill of the chase and of matchmaking between Thorn and Lady Lyte. Nothing gave Ivy quite the same sense of heady elation as playing Cupid on behalf of a man and a woman who were perfectly suited for one another but did not recognize it.

Swallowing the well-chewed food in her mouth, she

washed it down with a sip of ale. "Do you suppose there is any chance of them overtaking us?"

With the day waning, they had stopped in Gloucester just long enough to hire another coach, buy this food, and bribe an innkeeper to say they'd spent the previous night at his establishment, if anyone inquired.

"It's possible," Oliver admitted. "That barouche of my aunt's is a fine rig. With frequent change of horses, Aunt Felicity and your brother are bound to make good time. We must assume they will not be satisfied with lagging a day's ride behind us, either."

"But we aren't really a day's ride ahead." Why did her insides quiver like jelly at the notion of being caught and dragged back to Bath? Thorn would be vexed with her, of course, but he never managed to stay angry for long.

"I pray they don't find out how close we are." Oliver took a drink of his own ale. "Now that I am satisfied they are on our trail, I believe we should try to put more distance between us. If we drive through the night, morning should find us the better part of the way to Birmingham. It will not be a comfortable night's sleep, I fear …"

"I would be willing to suffer worse than a sleepless night on my brother's account," Ivy vowed.

At least that would spare them any bother about sleeping arrangements at an inn. When Oliver informed the landlord of the Green Dragon that they were newlyweds on their honeymoon tour, she must have blushed almost purple. The heat of that blush had spread from her face, all the way down her bosom and her belly, to her bottom. And that was before she'd experienced the reckless intensity of Oliver's kiss.

They ate the rest of their rolling picnic in companionable silence, now and then exchanging a look, but more often staring out the coach windows at the Vale of Gloucester's rich farm land.

"By midday tomorrow we should arrive at Trentwell," remarked Oliver as Ivy stowed the remains of their supper in the hamper. "That is Aunt Felicity's country house. We should be able to stop there long enough for a decent meal and a wash up. I can also collect some papers I left behind."

"Do you continue your research even during summers in the country?" asked Ivy.

Oliver nodded. "That is my real work. During the winters in Bath I play about with scientific inquiry in a variety of areas, but in the summers I concentrate on applied science. I have written a book on crop rotation and I am working on a formula for a new type of pottery glaze."

Though she did not find this practical research quite as engrossing as some of the scientific matters they had discussed the previous evening over dinner, Ivy still gave Oliver her undivided attention and prompted him with questions she hoped he would not consider too dim-witted. She found herself admiring the dedication he brought to his research. Oliver Armitage was not motivated by ambition for gold or glory, she sensed, but rather the noble ideals of mastering an intellectual challenge and finding ways to improve the livelihood of his neighbors.

Outside the coach, daylight slowly ebbed and a brisk wind swept up the Severn. Ivy pulled her shawl closer and closer around her.

Oliver paused in his explanation of porcelain manufacture. "Your teeth are chattering!"

Ivy clamped them together. "It is getting a bit ch-chilly, but I will be f-fine, truly."

"Nonsense." From out of the darkness his hand latched onto her arm and tugged her over onto the seat beside him. "They don't call this garment a greatcoat for nothing. It can easily accommodate the pair of us since we're neither very portly."

Ivy parted her lips to protest, but all that emerged was a sigh as the warmth of Oliver's coat enveloped her. How could she protest this necessary intimacy, when she'd already plunged them into potential scandal by spiriting the poor man off to Gretna?

"Th-thank you, Oliver." She snuggled against his torso, savoring the warmth of his arm around her shivering shoulders. "You have been far kinder to me th-than I deserve. I promise, though, I will make it up to you. Once Thorn and Felicity are happily settled, I'll do everything in my power to find you the perfect wife."

Their nearness and the subtle scent of him dispelled her chill in a way no quantity of blankets or bed-warming pans could have managed.

"What makes you think I need a wife?" She sensed a teasing note in his voice, so close to her ear. "Or want one, for that matter?"

For some reason, his second question left her vaguely unsettled. Perhaps that ham sandwich hadn't agreed with her.

"You may not *want* a wife," the tart reply burst out of her, "but, depend upon it, you require one to see to practical matters so you can concentrate on your work. And to keep you from starving yourself or going without sleep. Besides, don't you ever feel the need ... of a woman in your bed?"

The muscles of his arm stiffened, accompanied by a sharp intake of air. "Do you have any idea what you're asking?"

"I certainly do," she snapped. "Perhaps more than you, Mr. Nose-in-a-Book. My sister told me all about it once she got married. She did not want me going to my wedding night a poor green goose like she was. I'll admit I was a bit shocked by the information at first, but now that I've gotten used to the idea I believe it might be quite pleasant."

"Hmm ... yes ... well ..." The temperature inside Oliver's coat rose several degrees.

"Aren't you the least bit curious?" Ivy persisted.

Some wicked streak in her relished the opportunity to make Oliver Armitage squirm. It would serve him right for saying he didn't want a wife — as though women were, and would forever remain, superfluous to his monkish existence.

Why that should perturb her quite so much, Ivy could

not work out. Perhaps she understood less about matters of the heart than she had boasted to Oliver.

Chapter Five

WAS HE NOT the least bit curious?

On the contrary, Oliver Armitage had never burned so with curiosity about a subject. He'd heard enough to guess what must transpire when a man and a woman joined their bodies. He'd gathered there was physical pleasure involved, but he had never been able to reconcile himself to the sordid means by which most of his male acquaintances had satisfied their "thirst for knowledge."

Dashed if he would admit his ignorance to this brazen chit for her further amusement! Particularly when she roused his interest in the whole matter as no other female ever had.

Pointedly ignoring her question, he posed one of his own. "How would you describe this *perfect wife* you mean to find for me? And what makes you think such a paragon would want a tiresome fellow like me, other than to get her clutches on my aunt's fortune in due time?"

"I didn't say she would be perfect in the absolute sense, only perfect for *you*. And what makes you think she would only want you for your fortune? You have plenty of first rate qualities that any wise woman would prize above material considerations."

Ivy angled herself and tilted her face toward him. He could feel the whisper of her breath on his cheek. Oliver continued to stare straight ahead into the darkness. He did not trust himself to turn his lips in her direction.

"You are in the minority of your sex for thinking so, I fear. Or perhaps having been the target of more than one fortune-seeking woman has jaundiced my opinion of women."

Ivy pressed her head to his chest. If she meant it as a gesture of comfort, Oliver was surprised to discover it worked.

"I'm sorry if they hurt you. I can tell you from experience that being in straitened circumstances changes the way a lady must regard potential suitors. Many families pressure their daughters to make the most advantageous marriage, but that does not mean they would marry an odious man for his money. Only that they might have to give up a nice one if he had no prospects, as Papa made Rosemary do when my brother-in-law first began courting her."

Swathed in discreet darkness, Oliver permitted himself the hint of a smile. Earlier that day, during their headlong rush from Newport to Gloucester, Ivy had related all the particulars of her sister's second chance at love. By the sound of it, she had reason to be proud of her matchmaking skills. Would Rosemary Greenwood and Merritt Temple have found their way back to one another, Oliver wondered, without a blatant push from Rosemary's meddlesome little sister?

"The ideal Mrs. Armitage won't care a fig for your aunt's money," announced Ivy with reckless confidence. "She will have to be a bit of a bluestocking. That goes without saying, but not *all* prunes and prisms. Pretty but not band-boxy. A pinch of bossiness wouldn't hurt, to make certain you take regular meals and go to bed at a reasonable hour . . ."

She chuckled.

"What else?" Oliver demanded.

"I only thought it mightn't go amiss if she has the sort of attributes men fancy in women, so you would be glad to tuck into bed early."

"You are incorrigible!" Even as he joined in her laughter at her own expense, Oliver reflected on Ivy's description of his ideal wife.

He doubted the bluestocking part was necessary. Ivy Greenwood had demonstrated that a woman could have a keen mind and lively curiosity without being aggressively studious. He had a few other attributes he might add to her list as well. A loyal heart, a ready wit and an impish sense of fun to draw him out of himself.

It did not take a genius logician to recognize that only one young lady of his acquaintance answered that description. Might he be approaching this whole trip to Gretna from the wrong angle? Rather than using the time to work his attraction for Ivy Greenwood out of his system, perhaps he should set himself to win her.

Was it possible he could turn this mock elopement into the genuine article by convincing a certain charming matchmaker that *he* might be a worthwhile match for her?

⇒◆⇐

For the first time in her career of matchmaking, Ivy regarded an opportunity to play Cupid with decidedly mixed feelings. Describing the young lady she planned to locate for Oliver, she found herself resenting the future Mrs. Armitage.

Don't be a ninny! she scolded herself. *It's only because she is an abstract set of qualities, not an actual person.*

Yes, that must be it, she decided. When she met a real young lady who answered that description, no doubt "Miss X" would have a flaw or two to humanize her. Then Ivy would learn to like her without reserve and take genuine pleasure in watching her succumb to Oliver's courting … perhaps.

A deep yawn stretched Ivy's mouth so wide it ached. She had not slept well on that musty-smelling mattress at the Green Dragon. Oliver's firm chest made a much more satisfactory pillow. Her head lolled against him and her eyes slid shut.

"What about your ideal husband?" he prompted her. "Have you any plans to make a match for yourself?"

The words reached her right ear in the normal fashion, but the left one, pressed against his topcoat, heard a deeper echo transmitted through his flesh, accompanied by the brisk rhythm of his heartbeat.

"One of these days, perhaps," she replied in a drowsy murmur. "I haven't met him yet, but I will recognize him the moment I do. I have been dreaming of him for years, you see."

"Indeed?" Oliver heaved the word on a faint sigh, or did Ivy only fancy it from the foggy twilight of half-sleep? "Tell me all about him so I can keep a sharp eye out. Who knows but you may turn me into as incorrigible a matchmaker on your behalf as you are on mine."

Giddy with fatigue, the notion made Ivy chuckle. "I fear you would be a dismal failure in that regard, my friend. You would want a nice neat equation with all the figures tallied. Matters of the heart often go by contraries. Take my brother and your aunt for instance. You must admit, Lady Lyte is a rather unconventional woman."

"I would be the last to deny it." Oliver shifted in the seat, leaning back somewhat into the corner, making it even more comfortable for Ivy to rest against him. "I believe Aunt Felicity invited Thorn to become her lover, rather than the usual way 'round."

"It amazes me that he accepted." Fond thoughts of her brother flitted through Ivy's mind. "Though I adore him, I will be the first to admit Thorn is as conventional and responsible a solid citizen as you would meet in a fortnight. Yet, some special connection developed between him and Lady Lyte, in spite of their differences. How would the cold logic of science account for that?"

She heard and felt the laughter roll through Oliver. Both the sound and the sensation proved highly infectious.

"I would account for it by hypothesizing that opposites attract. It is a well-documented principle of magnetism. There may be more science at work in matters of the heart than you might suppose, Miss Cupid."

Opposites attract? That made a kind of sense. Weren't men and women opposites in many respects already?

"I will concede you that point, and I'll tell you all about the man of my dreams, though I doubt you will find his like among any of your acquaintance."

"And why is that?"

"Because he is rather wicked, Oliver. Does that shock you? A wicked, dashing rakehell with a dark past. My love will reform him, of course."

"Or his wickedness will corrupt you." Oliver's quip stung her with a barb of censure.

"Nonsense!" Ivy proceeded to spin a dramatic account of her imaginary suitor, though somehow her fantasy lacked its accustomed fire.

Gradually it sputtered out altogether as she subsided against Oliver, whose nearness made her feel warm in ways she'd never imagined.

———◆———

Though Ivy's presence in his arms heated Oliver's blood to an almost unbearable degree, her words chilled his heart. The assurance that she would never pursue him for his money was equally cold comfort. She'd made it clear that he was not, nor could he ever be, the kind of man she wanted for a husband.

To think otherwise would be deluding himself and a good scientist must never allow wishful thinking to impair his evaluation of the evidence. The way he'd once persuaded himself that his mother had not perished in the Indian Ocean, but miraculously washed ashore and would appear one day at his school and reclaim him.

Was Ivy Greenwood deluding herself with her romantic fancies? Oliver asked himself through that long night as he held her in his warming, protective embrace.

He did not for a moment believe the old adage about a good wife reforming the kind of wild young man Ivy had her heart set on. Her rakehell husband might be content until the novelty wore off, then he would revert to his true form and break Ivy's heart with his philandering. The way Uncle Percy had done with Felicity.

Why did he care anyway? Oliver's pride and logic scoffed. If the little fool wanted a scoundrel rather than a reliable but unexciting man of learning, no one had appointed him her keeper. He should have heeded his inner voice of caution and never let Ivy Greenwood charm her way past all the barricades he'd erected around his affections.

While their coach sped through the sleeping Worcestershire countryside, Oliver struggled to shore up his defenses and to subdue a mutiny by his body and his heart.

Chapter Six

"So *this* is Trentwell." Ivy pressed her nose to the coach window as it trundled down a wide lane canopied with lofty arching elms. "It looks so much grander than old Barnhill."

Oliver responded with an off-hand, dismissive sounding grunt. His vacant gaze did not stray from some fixed point off in the distance.

He must be deep in contemplation of some arcane chemical formula or complicated scientific theory, Ivy decided, for he'd been even quieter and more abstracted than usual all morning. She could hardly believe he was the same man she'd snuggled close to last night, exchanging confidences and easy banter. Today he exuded all the warmth and ease of a granite statue.

Might his behavior indicate more than intellectual pre-occupation? Had she said or done something to make him angry with her? Did he resent her well-meant intention of finding him a wife?

For the first time, Ivy pitied the future Mrs. Armitage. If she possessed a sensitive, affectionate nature, the poor young lady might well be grieved by the sort of chilly indifference Oliver had exhibited today.

Not that it mattered to Ivy in the least.

Oliver Armitage was simply her partner in this scheme to reunite Thorn with Lady Lyte. If she'd begun to fancy any more tender feelings toward him, it could only be due to the enforced intimacy of their journey. Ivy hoped the long carriage ride would have an even stronger effect of that nature on her brother and his mistress.

As for Oliver and her, they could obviously use some time apart, even a few hours. If her chatter grated on his sensibilities as his glacial silence grated on hers, Oliver would undoubtedly agree.

The coach slowed as it reached the end of the lane, which looped around a dainty marble fountain. Their approach had clearly been noted by Lady Lyte's remaining servants, for a middle-aged footman waited in front of the house to greet them.

"Why, Master Oliver, this is a pleasant surprise, sir." The man beamed when he recognized his employer's nephew. "What brings you away from Bath so soon?"

"The most agreeable of reasons, Dunstan." The forced heartiness of Oliver's tone made Ivy wince. "I am bound for Scotland to be married."

He climbed out of the coach with a gait as stiff as his manner had been all morning. "We shan't be staying long. Just a few hours to eat a decent meal, change clothes and stretch our limbs a bit. We will be on our way again before nightfall. Don't want to delay the happy day, you know."

"Indeed, sir." The footman appeared to be struggling to digest this surprising information. "Congratulations to you and your lady. I wish you every happiness. Will you be coming back this way to pass your honeymoon, Mr. Armitage?"

The question brought a furious blush to Ivy's cheeks, prompted by thoughts of she and Oliver engaged in some of the honeymoon activities Rosemary had described to her. It appeared to fluster Oliver, too, for he made no direct reply to the question, but pretended to fix all his attention on helping Ivy out of the coach. Afterward, he sputtered a brief introduction to the footman, disengaging his hand from hers at the earliest opportunity.

"Would you be so good as to unload our bags, Dunstan, then direct Miss Greenwood to a room where she can wash and change clothes before tea." As he issued his orders, Oliver's gaze flitted to Ivy and away again as if he felt obliged to look at her when he didn't much want to. "I shall go speak to the stable master myself about tending our hired rig and horses."

"Very good, sir." The footman accepted Ivy's portmanteau, which the coachman handed down to him. "This way if you please, miss."

After a parting glance in Oliver's direction, which he did not return, Ivy followed the servant through a magnificent entryway, up a massive staircase and down an echoing corridor hung with paintings. The still, immaculate elegance of the place subdued her usual sunny spirits, already clouded by Oliver's distant behavior.

Back in Bath the extent of Lady Lyte's wealth had not been so apparent. No wonder her nephew and heir had a bevy of debutantes throwing themselves at his head!

If Ivy had entertained any foolish romantic notions about Oliver Armitage, which she most emphatically did not, this evidence of his brilliant expectations would have been more apt to dampen her enthusiasm than foster it.

A door suddenly opened in front of the footman and a smooth, masculine voice inquired, "What's all this, then? Company? Oh, good. I have been starved for amusement."

A young man lounged against the doorframe, regarding Ivy with a dark, admiring gaze. For a moment she wondered if her fatigue-fogged brain had conjured him down from one of the old portraits on the walls. Sporting a black moustache and chin beard, the fellow looked more like a cavalier of King Charles' day than a gentleman of the Prince of Wales' Regency. Disheveled raven hair fell around his shoulders. The rumpled state of his shirt, breeches and waistcoat suggested they'd been slept in.

She had no right to hold that against him, Ivy decided. Her muslin gown must look a fright for precisely the same reason. She flashed him a comradely smile — one ragamuffin to another, out of place in these pristine surroundings.

The footman nodded toward Ivy. "This is Miss Greenwood, Master Rupert. She and Master Oliver are breaking their journey here on their way to Gretna Green."

"Is that so, by George?" The young man called Rupert let his dark eyes linger on Ivy's face with an obvious mixture of admiration and interest. "Who'd have thought old 'Books' would snare such a beauty?"

Ivy could not decide whether she was flattered on her own behalf or offended on Oliver's. Who was this fellow, anyhow? He obviously made himself at home here and the footman had addressed him as though he was a member of the family. But Oliver claimed he had no living relations apart from Lady Lyte.

Perhaps the question blazed on her face, for the young man's smile twisted into a mocking grin.

"Rupert Norbury at your service, Miss Greenwood." Performing an extravagant bow over her hand, he pressed his lips to it. "Or perhaps rather than using my mother's name, I should take to calling myself Rupert FitzPercy. I am the eldest of his late lordship's merry-begotten brood. Lady Lyte suffers my presence at Trentwell, particularly when she is not in residence herself. It makes a convenient spot to hide out when my creditors grow tiresomely insistent."

"It is a pleasure to meet you, Mister Norbury." It was, too, Ivy realized. A great pleasure to converse with a man who looked her in the eye when he spoke. A man who appeared to regard her as more than an inconvenient article of baggage. A man who answered in every particular to her dashing, wicked ideal.

"I regret we won't be much company for you. We've only stopped for a few hours. Oliver had some books and papers he wanted to collect since we were passing this way." She should make some reference to her fictitious engagement, Ivy's conscience prompted her.

"A great pity you can't stay longer." Rupert heaved a deep sigh. "Though I can hardly blame 'Books' for wanting to whisk you in front of a parson before some importunate fellow steals you out from under his nose."

Why did such an impudent bit of flattery not make her blush as red and hot as radishes, Ivy wondered, when any off-hand remark or chance touch from Oliver Armitage seemed to make her cheeks blister?

Before she could find a satisfactory answer, she noticed the footman standing there with her portmanteau, trying for all the world not to appear impatient.

"I must go make myself presentable to be seen in a house as grand as Trentwell." Ivy pulled a rueful face. "'Books'... I mean Oliver and I will be taking tea before we go. I hope you will be able to join us."

"A regiment of dragoons couldn't keep me away." Rupert Norbury bowed again. "Dunstan, after you've shown Miss Greenwood to wherever you're taking her, have someone bring me hot water. I could do with a bit of sprucing up before I dine with my cousin and his intended."

<hr/>

The fresh, beguiling trill of Ivy's laughter drew Oliver toward the more intimate of Trentwell's two dining rooms. At the threshold, he froze, his limbs and voice paralyzed by the sight of Ivy pouring tea for his *cousin* Rupert. The fellow looked as though he'd been engineered precisely to Ivy's specifications, with an extra dash of wickedness thrown in for good measure.

"What are you doing here?" The words burst from his mouth at last as he willed his feet to carry him into the room.

Ivy was seated at the head of the table with a fine porcelain tea service arrayed before her. Rupert sprawled in the seat to her right, leaning as close to her as possible without falling out of his chair.

At Oliver's peremptory interrogation, Rupert glanced up, fixing him with a lazy, mocking stare. "Really, 'Books', you must make an effort to address your betrothed with more courtesy. Miss Greenwood is taking tea with us, of course.

Wasn't that part of the reason you stopped here on your way to Scotland?"

"I wasn't referring to *her*." Making a determined effort to ignore the jeer, Oliver dropped heavily into the seat on Ivy's left. "I was talking about *you*. The last I heard, you were in Ireland."

"I was." Rupert turned his full attention back to Ivy, his gaze roving over her bare arms and slender neck in the most impertinent manner. "It didn't suit me, so back I came, like the prodigal ... son. Nobody has offered to kill a fatted calf for me, but at least I have a roof over my head."

Perhaps more importantly, access to Aunt Felicity's wine cellar. The unspoken words curdled on the tip of Oliver's tongue, but he swallowed them. He'd learned long ago the folly of rising to Rupert's baiting. Today, for some reason, Uncle Percy's natural son proved more difficult than usual to ignore.

"Sugar, my dear?" Ivy asked. "Cream? Lemon?"

For a moment Oliver did not realize she was addressing him.

"Ask him again, louder," Rupert urged in a tone of exasperated amusement laced with pity. "He is probably lost in some lofty thought, and —"

"Just lemon!" Oliver rapped out his reply.

With the silver tongs, Ivy deposited a sliver of pale yellow fruit into the steaming amber brew. Did she slide a covert glance sideways at Rupert as she handed the cup to Oliver? And did the line of her lips arch a degree or two at the corner in response to his outburst?

Let her laugh at him — let them both laugh! The last laugh would be his, since Oliver refused to care how Rupert preened for Ivy's attention or how she simpered for his.

Rupert plucked a dainty sandwich from the tray and popped it in his mouth. "Are you certain I cannot prevail upon you to stay on at Trentwell a little longer? I am starved for society, particularly the charming variety offered by the future Mrs. Armitage."

He regarded Ivy with an appreciative gaze so sticky sweet, Oliver expected it to draw flies.

Deep in his chest, Oliver's heart seemed to skip a beat at the sound of his surname applied to Ivy. In his temples, his pulse thundered as he watched Ivy and Rupert exchange a flirtatious glance.

"We must be off straight away." He tried to speak dispassionately, as if relating a bald fact of the matter.

Instead the words spat out of him. He sounded like a schoolboy, vexed at losing a few marbles, declaring his intention to quit the game.

He tried again. "I believe Aunt Felicity may be following us in an effort to prevent our marriage, so we must make all possible haste."

"Surely you could extend your visit another hour or two." Rupert addressed himself to Ivy. "Trentwell has some of the most beautiful grounds in this part of the country. They are at their best now. Really 'Books', it is quite unfeeling of you to bring Miss Greenwood here, then whisk her away before she's had a chance to see them."

"Oh, please, Oliver!" Both Ivy's hands clutched his before he had time to pull away. "Can we not take a stroll to stretch our legs before we set off again?"

This time her touch did not provoke a passing jolt of static, but the sustained galvanism of a voltaic pile battery. If he spent the next hour with her, ambling along the wooded paths perfumed with spring flowers, what sort of foolish nonsense might he end up spouting?

"Very well." He detached his hand from hers on the pretext of reaching for another sandwich. "Perhaps we ought to take a little exercise while we have the chance. I believe I shall row around the pond."

For an instant, Ivy looked as though she would ask to join him. Against all reason, Oliver found himself hoping she would.

Before she could frame that request or any other, Rupert

dove into the conversation again. "If 'Books' is going to be occupied at his oars, I should be honored to escort you on a tour of the grounds, Miss Greenwood."

Ivy hesitated, "Oliver?"

What did she want him to do — forbid her going off with Rupert when she was obviously so anxious to? Beg her to come out in the boat with him?

Not likely.

"Please yourself." Oliver made himself shrug, though his shoulders resisted the simple motion. "It is of no consequence to me. Just don't stray out of earshot so I can call you when it's time to leave."

Something in her blue-green eyes told him he'd given the wrong answer. But when he glimpsed Rupert's gloating grin, Oliver could not bring himself to retract his words.

Chapter Seven

WHAT SHE DID was of no consequence to him. What Oliver meant was that *she* was of no consequence to him.

Very well then, Ivy decided as she flounced out of the dining room on Rupert Norbury's arm. She would not allow Oliver's opinion to be of any consequence to her, either.

That was more easily said than done.

Somehow the fresh, sharp greens of spring foliage and the bright fragrant blossoms paled before her eyes, while small clouds collected to obscure the sun. Even Mr. Norbury's sparkling patter did little to lift the subtle weight oppressing her spirits.

"Tell me, my dear." He led her down a hedge-bordered path. "How on earth did you manage to woo a dry old stick like 'Books' into such a grand adventure as eloping to Scotland? I am dumbstruck that he was willing to risk Lady Lyte's displeasure, not to mention tear himself away from his tedious research for so long."

Even though she was vexed with Oliver, Ivy could not help resenting the fellow's mocking tone. "You are rather talkative for a man who claims to be dumbstruck, Mr. Norbury."

He threw back his head and laughed as though monumentally pleased with himself and with her. "Well played, Miss Greenwood! I concede the hand to you. I should have known my cousin would not saddle himself with a stupid wife, no matter how decorative."

If Rupert Norbury meant his comments for flattery, they

fell short of their target.

Through a gap in one of the hedges, Ivy spied the pond. Oliver had just pushed away from the bank in a narrow boat. He began rowing with smooth efficient strokes.

If only he'd given her a crumb of encouragement, she might be sitting in that boat now, too, lulled by the soft rhythmic dip of the oars and the tranquility of the lapping water.

Instead, she must suffer Rupert Norbury's animated prattle about card games won and lost, ridiculous lengths to which he'd gone to evade his creditors, and bits of scandalous personal gossip concerning the unprincipled set of people he considered his friends.

"... then Miss Deagle pushed Mrs. Forrest backward into the fountain, which fortunately was not deep. But when the poor creature rose from the water, of course, the drenched gown was plastered to her like a second skin, leaving ... I declare, Miss Greenwood, I don't believe you've heard a word I've said." A badly spoiled five-year-old could not have sounded more petulant.

He was correct though. Ivy had not been paying much mind to his conversation — if one could call it that when Rupert Norbury did practically all the talking. She had been more occupied with trying to avoid his hip brushing against hers so often. The sensation put her in mind of the time she'd trodden on an eel while wading in the brook near Barnhill. It sent a shiver through her, but not the pleasant kind she experienced when Oliver touched her.

"I beg your pardon. What were you saying?"

Oliver's cousin rolled his eyes skyward. "Perhaps you are a better match for 'Books' than I first thought, Miss Greenwood, with your wandering mind."

Was this how *her* conversation affected Oliver? Ivy cast a glance down the sloping lawn toward the pond. Did it strike him as so shallow and self-absorbed that he had no choice but to slam the door of his attention in her face then turn his mind to worthier subjects?

"I apologize for my preoccupation, sir." She let go of Mr. Norbury's arm and put a distance of several steps between them. "A bride may be forgiven, I hope, for letting her thoughts often stray to her future husband."

His pique forgotten, Rupert Norbury laughed until tears rolled from his eyes and he had to gasp for breath.

"I fail to see what you find so amusing." To Ivy's ears, his laughter held more scorn than merriment. She fumbled for an excuse to put more distance between herself and this odious man. "I believe I shall return to the house. The way the sky is darkening, I fear we may soon have rain."

As she skirted around him to go back the way they'd come, Mr. Norbury's hand whipped out and caught her by the wrist. "Pray, do not deprive me of your company so soon, Miss Greenwood. You haven't seen the fruit tree arbor yet."

She tried to shake off his hand, but Rupert Norbury hung on with a strength of grip that surprised her. He had fleshier hands than his cousin, Ivy realized, their skin softer than most women's. Had they ever done more strenuous work than rolling dice, tipping a wine cup, or peeling off a woman's clothing?

That last thought made Ivy's gorge rise.

"Kindly let go of me, Mr. Norbury. Viewing the arbor can wait upon a future visit to Trentwell."

If Thorn married Lady Lyte, Ivy was not certain she would want to visit Trentwell again, particularly if her ladyship's illegitimate stepson might be in residence.

"But the blossoms are at their peak, now." He pulled her toward him. "Who knows if you might catch them in such perfection again. 'Gather rosebuds, while you may.'"

"Mr. Norbury! Please stop!"

The midnight glitter in his dark eyes made the flesh on the back of Ivy's neck tighten. What childish folly had ever led her to believe there could be anything romantic or exciting about wickedness?

"You may drop your pose of sentimental devotion to 'Books'. If you are preoccupied with anything, it might be the notion of one day being mistress of Trentwell."

"I am *not* after Oliver's fortune." For some reason it felt more urgent to challenge that assumption than to protest Rupert Norbury's importunate grip on her.

"You mistake me, my dear. I don't hold it against you. Why, I have tried to spirit more than one young heiress off to Gretna in my day."

An uncharitable judgement of those young ladies' taste and intelligence crossed Ivy's mind, followed by a swift, stinging indictment of her own. She had been lured by his striking looks and glib allure. If she had not been acquainted with another sort of man — one who, despite his flaws, had genuine worth and ability — she might not have seen past Rupert Norbury's appealing facade so quickly.

"Having a husband who is so blind to your needs and charms can have its advantages, you know." He pulled her into his embrace. "'Books' is not likely to notice if you seek satisfaction elsewhere."

"Stop calling him that and let go of me!" Ivy struggled to break his grip.

Turning her face from his approaching lips, she almost retched at the loathsome sensation when he kissed her ear instead. She brought her foot down hard on his toes, but her flimsy slippers were no match for Mr. Norbury's riding boots.

"No need to play coy, now." The blackguard chuckled and tightened his grip further. "My dear cousin is too far off to hear us, not that he would pay much mind if he did. You and I are quite alike, Ivy. With me, you won't need to make any tiresome pretenses."

She wasn't anything like him ... was she? The hideous notion slapped Ivy into a moment's limp, stunned silence.

"Ah, that's better." Mr. Norbury accosted her bare neck with his lips. Between kisses that made Ivy's flesh crawl, he murmured, "I would never hurt you or force you, of course. And we haven't the time to indulge ourselves just now. I only want to give you a little foretaste of what awaits in the future."

Perhaps she should allow him to kiss her and paw her a little, thought Ivy. Endure it as a fit punishment for her stupidity. Oliver wouldn't care one way or another.

Somehow she could not let herself give Rupert Norbury the satisfaction of believing she preferred him to a man like Oliver. Feeling his grip slacken, she wrenched one hand free and scored his face with her nails. He bellowed a shocking oath and called her an even more shocking name.

Perhaps thinking she meant to scream, the rogue clamped a hand over her mouth with bruising force. Primal fury surged through Ivy. She bit down on one of his fingers, glorying in the howl of pain it provoked.

When he let her go, Ivy released his finger from her teeth and made a bolt for freedom. She'd scrambled only two steps when something checked her headlong rush. The bounder must have grabbed a handful of her skirt, Ivy realized as she pitched to the ground, the screech of tearing muslin filling her ears.

>◆<

Oliver strove to channel his anger and agitation into the force of his oars against the water. Perhaps the rhythmic, repetitive movement would soothe his overwrought emotions and distract his attention from the periodic glimpses of Rupert and Ivy through the hedges.

Why did the sight of them together poke his heart with sharp sticks? Surely it came as no surprise that Ivy would prefer his engaging, worldly, rascal of a cousin to him? Even if she had not professed herself disposed to a dashing, wicked young man, Rupert would have lured her.

If he had a crumb of sense left, Oliver knew he ought to thank his cousin for this harsh but necessary lesson about the folly of allowing emotion to ride roughshod over intellect. Scientific quandaries might baffle and frustrate him by times, but matters of the heart baffled and frustrated him *all* the time.

Unlike the austere, elegant realm of scientific theory and pure mathematics, the kingdom of Cupid could be messy, ugly and downright painful.

What were Ivy and Rupert up to now? For the three hundred and fifteenth time, Oliver assured himself their actions were of no consequence to him. Not even if they had stopped walking. Not even if they were standing so close together he could hardly tell if they were two people or one. Not even if they might be kissing.

Without noticing that he'd changed direction, Oliver found himself rowing toward them instead of away. Perhaps he had better interrupt their little tryst, after all.

The decision had nothing to do with his thwarted feelings for Ivy. He was responsible for her, though. In her naiveté, she might hanker for a rake like Rupert, but she deserved far better. If she could not exercise a little common sense in the matter, he would elect himself her voice of reason.

Oliver had almost reached the far bank of the pond when he heard his cousin roar a curse. In his haste to scramble ashore, he tipped the boat and tumbled into the pond. The cold water did not succeed in cooling his temper. He wallowed ashore and surged up the slope in time to hear Rupert cry out again.

When he reached the path an instant later, he found his cousin poised over Ivy, who had fallen to the ground, or perhaps been pushed. Her skirt and undergarment had both been torn from hem almost to waist. A breathtaking expanse of shapely leg protruded through the long slit.

Oliver's pulse throbbed in his forehead . . . and lower. For the first time in his adult life, he could not grasp the reliable rope of logic. Instead it slid through his fingers as if greased, leaving him swamped in the stormy seas of passion.

"Damn you, Norbury!" His breath heaved in and out in such gusts he could scarcely gasp the words out. "Get your . . . lecherous hands . . . *off* her . . . this instant!"

Rupert turned on Oliver with a sneer. "Stay out of this

'Books'."

Three red lines in parallel blazed on the wastrel's cheek. Taken together with his earlier loud cries, they suggested Ivy had not submitted tamely to his liberties.

Oliver's mind whirled in such a tempest of savage urges, he sensed himself all but incapable of rational thought. Instinct, potent and undeniable, demanded he protect the woman and punish any man who challenged him for her.

Forgetting that he had long disdained violence as the conduct of fools, Oliver grabbed his uncle's misbegotten son by the neck linen and wrenched him to his feet. Norbury flailed out with his fists, fetching Oliver a glancing blow to the stomach.

Though he doubled over for an instant, Oliver did not release Norbury's stock. If anything he gripped it tighter, holding his cousin's handsome, scornful face steady for the tightly clenched fist he slammed into Norbury's jaw.

The blow Oliver struck hurt his knuckles as much as the blow he'd taken pained his abdomen. When Norbury reeled back into the hedge, Oliver released his cousin's neck cloth, so he would not be dragged along. Some manner of blood-lust, completely foreign to his nature, raged in his veins urging him to beat his rival senseless. With enormous difficulty he resisted it, turning toward Ivy instead.

"Are you injured?" As he lifted her from the ground, Oliver yearned to wrap her in his arms and hold her for as long as she would let him, kissing away any residue of fear or pain.

A wave of queasiness seethed through his stomach. Perhaps it was a result of the blow he'd taken from Norbury. More likely it was guilt that he had left Ivy alone with his unprincipled cousin, because he'd been too much afraid of his own feelings for her.

Setting Ivy on her feet, he stepped back, crossing his arms in front of his chest to keep from reaching for her again. And as a token shield for his heart.

For the first time since he'd met her, Ivy Greenwood

looked thoroughly chastened.

"Injured?" She forced a gallant smile, which soon wavered then vanished. "Only my pride ... and my gown."

She shot a withering glance at Norbury as he struggled to extract himself from the shrubbery. "I just put on fresh clothes, too."

Oliver glanced down at his own sodden garments. "As had I. We shall have to change again as quickly as we can and get back on the road before Thorn and Aunt Felicity overtake us."

A look of dismay twisted Ivy's winsome features. She raised a quivering hand and pointed at something over Oliver's shoulder. "I fear we may be too late."

Why he even bothered to turn and look, Oliver could not fathom. He knew what he would see.

Pulled by two teams of hired horses, his aunt's barouche rolled up the stately drive toward Trentwell.

Chapter Eight

OLIVER TURNED BACK to Ivy. With the white linen of his shirt plastered to his chest and his arms crossed in front of him, he had never looked more attractive to her. Nor more forbidding.

"What should we do now?" he asked.

"What *is* there to do?" Ivy's shoulders slumped. The well-spring that fed her bubbling fountain of optimism had suddenly run dry and it was all her own fault. "They have caught us. We must give ourselves up, I suppose, and hope your aunt and my brother have had enough time to mend their quarrel."

She'd made such a dreadful muddle of everything, dragging Oliver halfway to Scotland on a fool's errand. They might have been safely on the road this very minute if she had not been engaged in her silly flirtation with Rupert Norbury.

As Norbury staggered to his feet, rubbing his jaw and looking terribly sorry for himself, Ivy knew she would never regard a handsome rakehell the same way again. Though part of her wanted to wilt into a puddle of petulant tears, she resolved to start acting like a grown-up. She owed Oliver that much, no matter how belated.

"I will tell your aunt I devised the whole scheme and you only accompanied me under protest, to prevent me from coming to harm." She would not have to stretch the truth on that point.

Oliver stood quite still, as if weighing her words. Then he held out his hand to her. "There may be another way. I have a plan, if you are willing."

"A plan?" A slender jet of hope shot in a high arc from Ivy's fountain. It splintered a stray beam of May sunshine into a hundred tiny rainbows. "Then let us pursue it, by all means."

She placed her hand in Oliver's. As his long deft fingers closed over hers, a sense of warm tranquility stole over Ivy much like she felt whenever she returned to Barnhill after a long absence.

"See here, Rupert," Oliver ordered his cousin. "Will you help us, or shall I tell Aunt Felicity and Ivy's brother what devilment you were getting up to with her?"

"Very well." Rupert Norbury pulled a sulky face. "What do you want me to do?"

More than Oliver's threat compelled him, Ivy felt certain. Perhaps the scoundrel hoped to nudge Oliver out of favor with Lady Lyte.

"Tell Aunt Felicity and Mr. Greenwood that we have gone for a stroll around the grounds and will not be back until supper," said Oliver. "Then load our luggage into a gig and bring it to the village. You will find us waiting at the Fox and Crow. Mind you're not spotted and followed, though."

Norbury made a show of dusting the tiny hedge leaves off his coat. "Don't be telling me my business, Books ... er ... Armitage. I've had more practice sneaking around than you'll ever have."

A fine thing to boast of! Ivy and Oliver exchanged a look, their brows arched.

"This way." Oliver tugged her down the hedged path toward a stand of trees. "I hope this will give us a few hours lead on them, if we can trust Rupert to carry out his part."

Ivy gave an exaggerated shudder. "He's horrible, isn't he?"

"You seemed to find him most diverting at tea time." Oliver let go of her hand as they entered the woods. "I thought he answered to the description of your ideal man in every particular. Perhaps you did not find him wicked enough. He's not, really ... just vain, selfish and irresponsible."

"You must think he and I make a perfectly matched pair."

Though Ivy tried to toss the words off as a jest, shame soured her tone. There wasn't anything funny about Oliver Armitage despising her.

"I think nothing of the sort." Oliver held back a sapling that barred the overgrown woodland path so Ivy could squeeze by. "I blame myself for allowing you to go off with him. I should not have done it, except ... that is ... I should have known better. I'm ... sorry."

She could not stand to see Oliver reproach himself for *her* imprudence. She would relieve his conscience of that burden, even if it meant exposing the sum total of her foolishness. Lobbing the words over her shoulder or addressing them to his back would not do, either. Ivy turned to face him, reluctant but determined to make a clean breast of the matter.

"You needn't blame yourself, Oliver." What business did she have making matches by manipulating other people's feelings when she'd been so blind to her own? "I went with your cousin for an even more ridiculous reason than because I thought I fancied him."

Oliver raked his long fingers through his wet hair and adjusted his spectacles, which had been knocked askew. He fixed her with the same bemused questioning gaze as when she first barged into his study and demanded he run away with her to Gretna. All the feelings he'd stirred in her since then deluged Ivy's heart in a bittersweet, bewildering tangle.

Curiosity, exasperation, respect, tenderness, pique, fascination, desire — and none of it with a hope of being returned, apart from the exasperation.

The young scientist could not think less of her than he did all ready, so she might as well tell him the whole humiliating truth. "You hadn't been paying me much attention, so I wanted to see if I could make you jealous. How's that for nonsense?"

Oliver did not reply at first. He stared at her as Ivy felt her self-confidence shrivel into a small but weighty lump in the pit of her stomach.

In the leafy canopy above them, birds warbled as if their

tiny bodies would explode with joy unless they released it in song. The aroma of May blossoms perfumed the still woodland air. The forest wore a spring mantle of lush, expectant green.

But in Ivy's heart a cold November drizzle settled over bare branches and brown, dead bracken. She longed to vent her feelings in a cleansing bout of tears, but that must wait until she was alone. She would not burden Oliver more than she had already.

━━◆━━

"I ... don't understand." Oliver gave his head a vigorous shake. He'd heard Ivy's words and he knew their individual meanings. Taken together, however, they refused to make sense for him.

Or perhaps the muted sparkle of Ivy's springtime eyes had driven all rational thought from his mind.

"You were *trying* to make me jealous?" She'd succeeded beyond any measure she could have intended. It had taken every ounce of restraint, cultivated over many years, to keep from pummeling Rupert's comely face to a jelly. "Why?"

Ivy pursed her lips in a rueful grin, but her eyes betrayed a hint of moisture. "If you cannot deduce that simple conclusion from the evidence, Mr. Armitage, I fear for your future as a scientist."

If she'd been speaking of any other man, he might have summed the equation with ease. "Y-you *care* something for me?"

"So it seems." A stray shaft of sunlight pierced the leafy canopy above, further gilding Ivy's riot of red-gold curls and her rapidly blinking lashes. "It took me long enough to figure out. I don't believe I've properly sorted it out yet. That does not speak well for my boast of understanding about love, does it?"

Ivy had admitted she cared about him. She'd even used the word love, however indirectly. That much Oliver could take in, though he still had difficulty believing it. What he could not fathom was why it made her look so woeful.

"Don't fret." She started to turn away. "I promise not to throw myself at your head for the rest of our journey. I am well aware that I do not answer the description of your ideal match."

The tiny catch in her voice acted like a key, unlocking Oliver from his confusion. Her feelings for him dismayed Ivy for the same reason he'd been alarmed by his mounting attraction to her — because she believed he could not return them.

Part of him wanted to sit down and puzzle it out. Weigh the facts. Make a well-considered decision. One that would not overturn his whole life the way his precipitous leap from the boat had capsized it.

As he wavered, Ivy took a few steps along the path and disappeared behind the thick trunk of a towering oak tree. All at once the sunlight seemed to lose its luster and the vibrant colors of the leaves grew dull.

"Wait!" Oliver rushed after her, almost tripping in his haste and not caring if he did.

Ivy glanced back, prompted perhaps by the sound of his hurried footsteps. A delicious expanse of her bare leg protruded through the tear in her skirt. Her hair had captured a few stray leaves — an emerald chaplet fit for a queen of the woodland nymphs.

His longing for her must have blazed on his face. Whatever she saw lit an answering smile in Ivy — one so bright and warm it eclipsed the spring sunshine.

Somehow Oliver knew this was not the time for questions, discussion or words of any kind. Instead he scooped Ivy up and spun her around, setting his head in a dizzy whirl to match his heart.

As his arms closed around her and his lips sought hers, a whisper of doubt chilled him as surely as a stray breeze over his wet clothes. Would Ivy welcome such an ardent demonstration of his feelings so soon after Rupert had forced his odious attentions upon her?

Before Oliver had time to recant his rash action, Ivy's arms closed around his neck. Her lips greeted his in an eager kiss that distilled all the green, fragrant promise of spring.

She was his springtime, Oliver realized — unpredictable, vivacious, romantic, invigorating. The gentle rain of her sympathy and the clement sunshine of her temperament had chased cold, barren winter from his heart and nourished the fragile seed of his fancy for her.

When they paused to catch their breath, Ivy pressed her brow to his until all he could see were those turquoise pools he longed to immerse himself in at the start of every day.

Her slender body vibrated with laughter. "If you are bewitched, Oliver Armitage, I must warn you, I shan't make the least effort to locate an antidote."

"Oh, I am bewitched, Lady Cupid." A week ago, he would have sneered at any fool who mouthed such fanciful drivel. Now he pitied anyone whose life was uncolored by a little romance. "You cast a spell on me the moment you barged into my study and demanded I run away with you to Gretna Green. I have fought against it with every weapon of logic at my disposal, but you have vanquished them all."

"Well, I have learned a little wisdom to temper my romantic fancies." She rubbed her pert little nose against his straight jutting one and lavished him with a look of bewitching impudence. "Only a very little, mind. Enough to recognize that you are as dashing and masterful as any rogue. But a good deal more interesting and congenial once the shallow gilding of glamor has worn off."

"In that case ..." Oliver set Ivy on her feet again and dropped to his knees before her. "... my very dear Miss Greenwood, would you do me the honor of becoming my wife once we reach Gretna?"

No one in Oliver's recollection had ever looked at him with such transparent adoration. He wondered if, like the songbirds, his chest might burst from the happiness swelling inside him.

"Indeed, I will," whispered Ivy. Her lower lip trembled for an instant then twisted into an impish grin. "Provided you don't come to your senses before then."

Oliver pulled her toward him, nestling his cheek against the soft bounty of her bosom. "If you perceive any danger of that happening, I hope I may count on you to kiss me senseless again."

"That I shall." She chuckled, nuzzling her cheek against his damp hair. "Now, much as I hate to be the one to bring up practical matters, we had better get ourselves to that Fox and Crow establishment where you told Rupert to bring our luggage."

With a grudging nod Oliver surged to his feet. Much as he would have liked to linger in the woods with his pretty nymph, they would now have a perilously slender lead on Thorn Greenwood and Aunt Felicity. For the remainder of their journey, he and Ivy would be fleeing headlong toward Gretna Green in earnest.

Chapter Nine

"CARLISLE, AT LAST." Ivy sighed as their coach rattled past the crumbling ruin of Hadrian's Wall. "One more change of horses should see us to Scotland."

"Not far now." Oliver roused from his restless doze and let his right hand stray from Ivy's shoulder down her arm. "Soon we shall be husband and wife."

As his hand veered inward to graze over the subtle rounding of her bosom, a sound issued from his bride-to-be, like the purr of a contented kitten. When she nuzzled her cheek against his chest and rubbed her hand over the too-sensitive flesh of his thigh, Oliver gained a very personal understanding of the heat produced by friction. If he did not kiss Ivy immediately, he feared his whole body would burst into open flame.

The way she snuggled against him made it impossible to engage her lips without a series of contortions to which his spine was quite unequal. Instead, he seized her and spun her around, landing her deliciously rounded bottom onto his lap. Her head tilted over his arm in the perfect posture for kissing.

As their lips met and mingled and a blast of delicious heat surged through his body, Oliver wondered if there could be a better way to begin every day for the rest of his life.

⇒━◆━⇐

Had she ever imagined Oliver lacking in passion? Ivy marveled at her own ignorance. Perhaps the angels did watch over well-meaning souls whose good intentions outstripped their good sense, she decided as she clung to Oliver. Certainly she'd been blessed beyond anything she deserved.

"The minute we are safely married, I shall haul you away to some inn for a hot meal." She ran her fingertips over his lean unshaven cheek. "I may not possess many practical skills of a good wife, but I have mastered cookery. So I serve you fair warning — you have missed your last meal, sir. From now on, I will make it my mission to keep you well nourished."

He raised her hand to his lips and swiped them across her knuckles. "You are talking like a wife, already. If you keep it up, I shall find myself calling you Mrs. Armitage."

Oliver might have meant to tease her, but Ivy heard the barely suppressed longing in his voice. Clearly he wanted precisely the kind of looking after she yearned to give him.

"Just think." Ivy yawned and stretched. "By tonight we will be married, we'll have eaten our first hot meal in days and we will get to sleep in a proper bed rather than sitting up in some drafty, rattling old coach."

A hint of emerald devilment glittered in Oliver's luxurious hazel eyes as he caressed her bosom through the light fabric of her bodice. "I hope you aren't counting on getting too much sleep on our wedding night. I am anxious to discover all the intriguing information your sister imparted to you."

A sound broke from Ivy's lips — a whimper of desire roused but unsatisfied. "For a sober man of science, you have demonstrated lamentably passionate tendencies in the past day or two."

She pulled his face toward hers for another kiss. A kiss she'd come to know and enjoy and crave ever since their precipitous flight from Trentwell. Lost in that deep, passionate kiss, neither she nor Oliver took much notice as their coach slowed and stopped.

Then the door of the vehicle was wrenched open and a familiar gruff voice thundered, "I suggest you take your hands off my sister, Mr. Armitage!"

"Thorn!" For the first time in her life, Ivy wanted to

bludgeon her beloved brother. "What are you doing here?"

"Spoken as if you had no idea," Thorn growled. Seizing Ivy by the arm, he hauled her out of the coach and onto the cobble-stones in front of a prosperous-looking inn. "Have you made it your mission in life to turn me gray-headed before I'm forty?"

Ivy had never seen her brother so angry. His deep brown eyes, usually so calm and steadfast now flashed with dark fury. That look made her want to crumple before his displeasure, like a naughty six-year-old caught at dangerous mischief.

Then she felt Oliver's hands close over her shoulders. The warm resonance of his voice enveloped her. "Do not be angry with your sister, Mr. Greenwood. The responsibility is mine."

Thorn cast Oliver a scathing glare. "I have plenty of outrage to go around, Mr. Armitage. You will come in for your share, never fear. I am hardly surprised to discover my sister up to such hijinks, but I had credited you with better sense."

Twisting her arm out of her brother's grip, Ivy traded him glare for vexed glare. "I will not permit you to speak to my fiancé in that tone, Thorn. Kindly apologize at once."

"That young man is *not* your fiancé and I will speak to him in any tone ..." Suddenly aware of the curious stares his tirade had drawn, Thorn swallowed his last words.

"Is Lady Lyte with you?" asked Ivy. Perhaps if Thorn understood what had set them on the road to Gretna, he might not be so angry with them.

"She is." His tone considerably subdued, Thorn nodded toward the inn. "Let us go inside and see what she has to say to the pair of you."

Thorn sounded so ominous. A choking lump of shame rose in Ivy's throat. She clung to Oliver's hand as they entered the inn and mounted the stairs behind her brother, meek as mice. When Thorn opened a door and ushered them through, Ivy guessed how a condemned criminal must feel on her way to the gallows.

As they stepped into a small sitting room, Felicity Lyte

rose from her chair by the hearth. She looked different than when Ivy had last seen her. Her face had lost flesh — hardly surprising if she and Thorn had been living on a diet of cold pies and sandwiches as Ivy and Oliver had.

There was more to it than that, though, unless Ivy was very much mistaken. Lady Lyte gave the impression of a woman who had drunk deeply from the cup of happiness, yet feared to drain it in case she might discover poison in the dregs.

Thorn shut the door then moved to stand behind Felicity. Beneath his severe scowl of brotherly censure, Ivy glimpsed a befuddled grin, barely held in check.

"It worked!" she cried, hurling herself upon her startled brother and his equally bewildered mistress. "I knew it would. I just knew it!"

She kissed Felicity on the cheek then threw her arms around Thorn. "I told Oliver if you were cooped up together in a carriage all the way to Scotland you would soon realize how much you cared for one another. And you did, didn't you?"

Oliver's aunt drew back from her impetuous embrace, staring at Ivy as if she was a lapdog who'd just messed on the floor. "Do you mean to say, you *planned* all this? Did you not have any intention of marrying my nephew?"

"Not at first." Something about the other woman's curt tone and stiff posture troubled Ivy, but she was too elated by the success of her matchmaking to pay it any mind. "It all started as a ruse to bring the pair of you together, but one thing led to another ... and ..."

Lady Lyte fixed Thorn with a horrified accusing stare. "You were in on this as well, weren't you? Did you put them up to it? I cannot believe I was gullible enough to let you twist me around your finger this way."

Pushing past his sister, Thorn tried to reason with his mistress. "I knew no more of it than you did, I swear. Surely you cannot believe I would stoop to such a thing."

"Keep your distance!" Shrinking back from him, Lady Lyte looked ready to vomit. "Don't *touch* me!"

If the woman he loved had hurled vitriol in his face, the acid could not have eaten into Thorn's flesh as viciously as her caustic suspicion seared his spirit. Even as Ivy's temper flared on her brother's behalf, she could feel the distress that radiated from Oliver's aunt.

Lady Lyte turned away from Thorn and Ivy as if she could not bear to look at them. Her anguished gaze fell on Oliver.

She held out her hand to him. "I do not hold you to blame for any of this, my dear boy. We have been abominably used, both of us. Just take me home … please."

———⊰◈⊱———

Oliver stood there, trying to make sense of what had happened so quickly. Like Ivy, he had sensed a renewed attachment between Thorn Greenwood and his aunt, beneath their displeasure over the elopement. For reasons that baffled him, Felicity's feelings for her lover had undergone a sudden shift in polarity. What had formerly attracted now appeared to repel with a vengeance.

"Please don't be angry with Ivy," he begged his aunt. "She only wanted to make the pair of you happy. And her brother knew nothing about it, of that I can assure you."

He could tell Felicity was not listening. Could he find the words to convince her when all he knew of love he'd learned in the space of a few short days?

"I know this has all fallen out like a comedy of errors, but that will not signify if we can give it a happy ending. Won't you and Thorn come with us to Gretna and make it a double wedding?"

The glow of perfect admiration on Ivy's face elated him even as the hurt and rage in his aunt's eyes cast him down.

"You foolish boy! Can't you see she is just like all the others — after you for *my* fortune?"

His aunt's accusation boxed Oliver in the stomach, driving the wind out of him. Could it be true? Experience insisted that it must.

But this was no orderly scientific experiment, where repeated results supported or refuted a theory. Love retained an element of sweet, capricious mystery. His own Lady Cupid had taught him that lesson.

"All evidence to the contrary, I believe Ivy loves me, Aunt Felicity. And I know I love her." He turned to Thorn Greenwood. "Will you please permit your sister to marry me, sir? I promise to do everything in my power to make her happy."

Ivy took her brother's hand. "Oh please, Thorn — please say yes! Don't do to me what Father did to Rosemary by forbidding her to wed Merritt."

Clearly Thorn Greenwood had trouble denying his sister anything she'd set her heart on. "I suppose … if the two of you have made it all this way without killing one another …"

"I cannot believe this," cried Felicity. "Don't tell me you mean to indulge this silly whim of theirs, after everything we went through to stop them? If you ever had the least genuine feeling for me, Hawthorn Greenwood, you will forbid this match and fetch your sister back to Barnhill, where she belongs."

Though his countenance remained impassive, something in Thorn's eyes betrayed the bitter tug-of-war taking place within him. "If you have the least feeling for me, Felicity, you will not ask me to sacrifice my sister's happiness."

He looked from Ivy to Oliver and back again. "If the pair of you are set on getting married, I will give the bride away."

Felicity flinched as if Thorn had struck her. "You are all in league against me, I see. Very well, then. If you persist in this folly, Oliver, I shall have no choice but to cut you off without a penny. See if *that* does not change Miss Greenwood's inclination to marry you."

The notion of giving up full time research in order to earn a living dismayed Oliver less than Ivy's crestfallen demeanor. Could Aunt Felicity be right, after all? Would Ivy be willing to wed a man with no prospects whatsoever?

Chapter Ten

ONCE AGAIN, SHE had made a muddle of everything. From the giddy heights to which they'd risen, Ivy's spirits plummeted.

One thing she would not spoil, whatever the cost to herself — Oliver's future.

"May we have a few moments' privacy to talk this over?" she begged Thorn and Felicity.

"Take as long as you like." Lady Lyte stalked toward the door. "I shall wait in my barouche for ten minutes. If Oliver does not join me by then, I will return to Bath without him and instruct my solicitor to write him out of my will."

When she had gone, Thorn looked from Ivy to Oliver. He seemed on the point of saying something then he shook his head and left the room.

The door had barely closed behind him when Oliver spoke. "What do you say, Miss Greenwood? Would you consider marrying a man with only his brains to recommend him?"

He was not going to make this easy for her, but Ivy knew what she had to do, no matter how distasteful. "You have far more to recommend you than just your brains, Oliver Armitage. If I had only myself to consider, I would be happier than ever to marry you without a penny to your name. That way, you would know for certain it is you alone I care for, not your expectations."

"That's settled then." He made a move to gather her into his arms. "You have made me the happiest pauper in the world! Let's join your brother and head for Gretna."

"No." Ivy had never done anything harder in her life than speak that word and step out of Oliver's embrace. "I will not be the cause of you losing your inheritance and perhaps having to give up your research. Your work is important, to you and to the world. Who knows what you might discover or invent? I am not used to putting anyone else's interests above my own, and it is not very pleasant I can tell you. But I care for you in a way I've never cared for anyone else."

She turned to the room's single tiny window, fearing the plea in Oliver's eyes might demolish her resolve. "I am not saying we must part forever. Only for a while, until your aunt comes to realize that we are right for each other. You must see this is the sensible thing to do. For once — for *you* — I want to be sensible."

Not hearing his footsteps behind her, Ivy started when his arms closed around her and Oliver spun her into his embrace. Had she ever thought him a cold, dispassionate fellow? His kiss shattered that foolish notion.

"Your proposal is entirely rational," he agreed, "but you have shown me that the most rational course is not always the wisest. I can and will find a way to continue my research without Aunt Felicity's support. What I cannot and will not do is postpone my happiness a moment longer. I have waited for it far too long. So long, I almost didn't recognize it when you barreled into my study and hauled me off on the adventure of a lifetime."

"Please do not deny me in this." Ivy pushed him toward the door. "It is hard enough to do the right thing when half of me doesn't want to."

"Give me one last kiss," Oliver entreated her. "Then I will do whatever you bid me."

"One kiss," Ivy wailed, "and I may not have the will to bid you do anything but marry me."

"That is what I'm counting on," whispered Oliver as he lifted her off the floor. His lips brushed across hers with the lightest of touches, gradually increasing in pressure and heat until they seared her memory of everything but pleasure.

When he set her on her feet again, lightheaded and breathless, her body on fire, it was everything Ivy could do to gasp, "Go with Lady Lyte."

A look of boyish mischief crossed Oliver's angular features. "Too late for that, I'm afraid." He picked Ivy up again and danced her across the room to the window. "That is her barouche just rounding the market cross. You are stuck with me now, Miss Greenwood."

"Monster!" Ivy planted a kiss on the tip of his nose. "Darling monster, you played me for time."

Oliver nodded. "I do not repent it for a moment and you must not either. It is only what you would have done if our positions had been reversed."

How could she deny it? "I shall be obliged to make you a very dutiful wife, to compensate for all you've given up on my account. Fortunately, I cannot think of a task I would rather undertake. Now let's go find my brother and fetch him to Gretna Green with us."

<hr/>

Oliver and Ivy Armitage were married later that day by the local vicar, for Thorn Greenwood refused to countenance any ceremony performed by Gretna's notorious *anvil priests*.

As Oliver stood beside his bride in the little Scottish church, speaking the vows by which lovers had sealed their union for hundreds of years, he thought back over the precipitous tide of events that had borne him there. Reason could scarcely grasp, let alone explain, the sudden radical shift in direction his life had taken. Perhaps there was something to that fanciful nonsense about Cupid and his arrows, after all.

"With this ring, I thee wed …" He slipped his own signet ring onto Ivy's finger, privately vowing to replace it with something suitably precious and delicate as soon as he could afford to.

As the vicar intoned the final benediction, Oliver had to gnaw on his lower lip to keep from exploding with laughter. How had he ever convinced himself of the preposterous notion that a trip to Gretna would purge Ivy from his system?

They signed the marriage register with Thorn and the vicar's wife as their witnesses then Ivy's brother drew Oliver aside for a few private words. "Be patient with her tonight, my boy, and treat her gently."

Apparently satisfied with Oliver's assurances, Thorn softened his gruff manner. "Once you get back to England, the two of you are welcome to make your home at Barnhill for as long as you need or wish."

Barnhill — that name made Oliver's expressions of gratitude catch in his throat. Not only would marriage to Ivy color his black and white world, it would also make him part of a family. And what could he give her in return?

"I promise you ..." He found his voice again, and with every word it rang stronger and more assured. "I will do everything in my power to make certain Ivy never regrets her decision to wed me."

Thorn held out his hand. "Do that, and I will be proud to call you my brother. Now, I must go. Ivy insists I make certain your aunt does not come to any harm on the journey south ... even if I am obliged to watch over her from a distance."

Ivy appeared at Oliver's side. "You had better be on your way if you're to have any hope of overtaking Lady Lyte." She embraced her brother and kissed him soundly on the cheek. "Take care of yourself, Thorn, and don't fret about me. I am in capable hands."

Oliver wished he felt as confident as his ever-hopeful bride appeared to be. He looked forward to their wedding night with a degree of fevered eagerness matched only by his sickening apprehension.

They dined at a nearby inn, recommended by the vicar as a respectable establishment. Though glad to eat his first proper meal in days, and half-inclined to linger over their supper to postpone their bridal rites, Oliver found himself with little appetite. Besides, he did not trust an overindulgence of food and wine on his churning stomach.

Their bed chamber turned out to be a vast improvement over the musty little cupboard in Newport — modest but snug and clean.

Before his doubts had an opportunity to steal through the door behind them, Ivy slammed it shut and hurled herself into Oliver's arms. The soft pressure of her lips against his and the sweet, familiar taste of her kiss whetted his anticipation and banished any misgivings.

"You are not having second thoughts or cold feet, or any awful regrets, are you?" she asked. "This is absolutely your last chance to back out. If we don't do all the things Rosemary told me about, I believe you might be able to have our marriage annulled. Then, after a little groveling, Lady Lyte would surely reinstate you as her heir." A small wistful cloud threatened Ivy's perpetual sunshine.

"Get one fact through your copper-curled head, Mrs. Armitage." Oliver hoisted her into his arms and strode to the bed. "You are worth more to me than Aunt Felicity's fortune. Furthermore, I suspect that value to increase manyfold upon longer and ... closer acquaintance."

Settling her on the bed, he showered every inch of her face and neck with kisses, prompting a trill of silvery giggles.

If I have any misgivings," he assured her, "they are on *your* account, not my own. Wouldn't you rather spend your wedding night with some dashing rogue who knows his way around a woman's body as well as he knows the green baize tables?"

"On the contrary, Mr. Armitage." Ivy set about untying his neck linen with nimble fingers. "I much prefer the prospect of a lover inclined to *experiment* in the science of pleasure."

Put that way, it did sound vastly intriguing. For the first time he could recall, Oliver crowed with laughter. "I must admit, I have a more than intellectual curiosity to explore that field of study."

He pried off his boots and flung his coat on the floor. "That is, if I can persuade you to assist me in my research."

His bride proved a most eager partner as they shed their clothes, turn-about and commenced to explore the intriguing differences in male and female anatomy.

Their avid curiosity led them to investigate effects of friction. Her fingertips over his thigh. His tongue, moist and hot, over the sensitive tip of her breast. All the while a sensation of heat and urgency intensified within and between them, like the pressure of steam in an engine boiler.

When Ivy whispered her sister's instructions for the coupling that would consummate their union, Oliver chuckled. "Precisely like a piston and cylinder. I shall blush whenever I see a steam engine after — oh, my!"

Science and intellect dropped to the floor with his discarded clothes. Oliver gave himself up, body, mind and heart to the primitive enchantment that drummed in his veins with a cadence of surging fire. Even as it heightened all his senses, it seemed to waft his consciousness out of his body.

Now he understood Thorn Greenwood's warning to treat his bride with patience and gentleness. His tender feelings for her bolstered his waning self-control, until she gasped his name and squirmed beneath him. The slick fiery grip of her body on his detonated an explosion of pleasure that hurtled him blazing into the stratosphere.

That violent convulsion of ecstasy gave way to an echo of downy, buoyant bliss. His arms wrapped around Ivy in a protective embrace, he rested his cheek against her moist, tousled curls and drifted toward sleep.

Ivy grazed her knuckles over his chest. "Do you have any regrets, now that it is too late to back out?" she teased.

Contorting himself to reach the sensitive flesh of her neck just below her ear, Oliver flicked his tongue over it. "If you can even ask such a question, you must not have been paying very close attention."

She wriggled as laughter bubbled out of her. "I will admit I was rather preoccupied with my own enjoyment."

"Then, to answer your question, I do not have a single regret in the world for us. It does grieve me that we did not accomplish our original purpose in coming here — to reunite your brother and Aunt Felicity. Like you, when I first saw them together, I believed we'd been successful."

Ivy nodded. "There is something troubling your aunt that has nothing to do with my brother, or very little at least. Never fear, though, I am not done matchmaking for those two yet."

With a fond chuckle Oliver kissed her again. Though he only meant it for a brief benediction, the delightful interplay of their mouths threatened to rekindle his desire.

"Now that I have an intimate understanding of what they are missing," he murmured, "you may count on me to be your willing accomplice in matchmaking, Lady Cupid."

The End

www.ingramcontent.com/pod-product-compliance
Lightning Source LLC
Chambersburg PA
CBHW020333130626
46549CB00003B/1151